FOR CASSIUS,
MAYOWA,
ROSE AND
MICAH

1

As soon as the school bell rang, Trey and Jax raced to their street dance rehearsal. Neither of them suspected that a cataclysmic, life-changing event was just around the corner. Cataclysmic, life-changing events simply didn't happen in a place like this.

Park View High School on a Tuesday afternoon had "normal" stamped all over it. If you looked up the word "normal" in the dictionary, you might just find a picture of the grey concrete schoolyard right beside it.

Looking boringly normal.

Trey waited for his little brother by the benches in the schoolyard. Jax was late. Like normal.

Jax eventually turned up and greeted his big bro with a punch on the arm. "All right, big man?" The sleeves of his over-sized school blazer dangled past Jax's wrists. Mum said he'd grow into it, but it was already May. He looked like he'd been forced into Trey's cast-offs.

Where was this growth spurt everyone said Jax was due? He was sick and tired of being the shortest boy in Year Seven.

Although Trey was lanky and Jax was pint-sized, they were instantly recognizable as brothers. They both shared the same light-brown skin that tanned to a deep brown at the first hint of sunshine. And thanks to regular barber trips with Dad, their thick brown hair was always trimmed to razor-sharp perfection.

Trey rubbed the sore spot on his arm. "Oi!

Save that energy for rehearsal."

They made their way to the PE hall like they did every Tuesday (except for the ones when Jax was in detention).

"Yo, Jax. Please tell me you turned in your French homework today?" Trey asked.

Jax waved his hand dismissively. "I'll get round to it."

Trey narrowed his eyes at Jax. "Because if it's late again, Mr Camembert will give you detention, and—"

"Heard you the first time, bro!" Jax interrupted. "Besides, I know all the answers. It'll take me ten minutes, tops."

"Oh yeah?" Trey smirked. "Ask me a question in French, then."

Jax stopped walking. He thought long and hard for several seconds. "Ummmm. Oui?"

Trey couldn't help but burst into laughter. "Just make sure that homework gets finished tonight, Jax. We can't afford to miss you for another rehearsal. Your Applejacks need work," he smirked.

"Tyrone! Jackson!"

Trey and Jax stopped in their tracks. Only one teacher at Park View High School always got their names wrong.

It was Mr Crankshaw, although half the school called him "Stankshaw" when his back was turned. And he was frowning so hard that even his giant bushy monobrow looked angry. The deputy head had an eerie ability to sense when a student was about to have fun on school grounds.

Laughing too hard? Nose not glued to a textbook? Daring to chat during one of his snoozefest geography lessons? Then Mr Crankshaw would be in your face quicker than you could say "tectonic plates".

Mr C had had it in for Trey and Jax since day

one. He'd called their parents for everything from uniform infractions (the school jumper had to be royal blue, not navy blue) to "inappropriate" hairstyles. And now it seemed that Jax was in for the same treatment. It felt so unfair.

"Sir, my name's Trey and my brother's name is Jax," Trey said patiently. How hard could it be to remember two names?

"Why are you boys loitering after home time?" Mr Crankshaw sneered. "I don't imagine you're staying late at the library?"

Trey sighed. Here we go.

Logan, the rugby team captain, seemed to appear out of nowhere. He stood next to Mr Crankshaw and peered down at the brothers.

"Sir, one of them's wearing trainers!" Logan said. "Isn't that against the rules?"

It was one thing being told off by a teacher. But when the school bully gets involved? That violates an unspoken rule of the playground.

Mr Crankshaw peered down at Jax's feet. "Right you are, Logan. Jackson, do explain why you're wearing leisure shoes on school grounds."

"I'm on my way to rehearsal with Fly High Crew, and—"

"A crew? You mean there's more of you?!" Mr Crankshaw spluttered. The angrier he got,

the more his giant monobrow wiggled like a furry grey caterpillar.

"Oh, there are loads of them," Logan said. "They play loud music and make a right mess of the PE hall. I've seen it with my own eyes, Sir!"

"This is most irregular, I must say," Mr Crankshaw huffed. "Thank you for the information, Logan."

A shark-toothed grin spread on to Logan's face. "Any time, Sir," he said before sidling away.

Ignoring Logan, Trey stepped in front of his little brother. "I can explain, Mr Crankshaw. Fly High Crew is our street dance squad, and we practise after school on Tuesdays. Other people use it to practise gymnastics, trampolining, martial arts … all sorts. Ms Tackle supervises!"

Jax looked at his brother proudly. Trey had petitioned their PE teacher, Ms Tackle, to let them use the PE hall. Thanks to him, kids at school like Trey and Jax finally had a real space to master their skills.

Sure, it was a tight squeeze and not a session went past without a squabble. The gymnasts grumbled about the street dancers' hip-hop. The street dancers had it in for the trampolinists, who took up way too much room.

It wasn't perfect, but it was theirs. Just as long as Mr Crankshaw kept his nose (and giant bushy monobrow) out of it. If he saw how much fun they were having, he'd ban it for sure.

"Hmph. Cartwheels won't help you pass exams. You'd do well to put homework first, Tyrone," Mr Crankshaw said.

"For the last time, his name is Trey! How would you like it if I called you Mr Stankshaw?!" Jax blurted out.

Mr Crankshaw's face went redder than a chilli pepper.

Trey gulped. Jax had gone too far.

But Mr C didn't scream, shout or threaten Jax with detention for the rest of his days. His eyes narrowed. "You and your little gang are going to regret that," he said quietly. Then he went back inside the school.

"We're not a gang," Trey muttered. "Since when does dancing after school make us a gang?"

Crankshaw would have no choice but to eat his words when Fly High Crew took first prize at the annual Summer Talent Show at the end of term.

Trey didn't set up Fly High Crew just so he could do a few backflips. Oh, no.

He had big plans for his squad. Like, colossal.

And it all started with making sure Fly High Crew was the BADDEST, the GREATEST and most EXCEPTIONAL street dance troupe in town.

"He's jealous of our moves. Stankshaw must be

the stiffest man in the entire universe," Jax said. "What sound do you think his knees make when he bends? Bet they go snap, crackle and pop!"

The boys fell about laughing. They felt a bit better already.

"Come on, joker," Trey said. "Less laughing, more practising."

That trophy wasn't going to win itself.

2

The brothers entered the PE hall to find the other athletes warming up. Trey took a deep breath, taking in the odour of rubber mats and the faint whiff of bleach used by the school caretaker. It wasn't a nice smell exactly, but Trey loved it. It reminded him that school was over and rehearsals were about to begin. The boys had already ditched their school uniform, swapping ties and shirts for T-shirts and trackies.

Trey and Jax had always loved dancing (their

mum insisted that they could both body-pop before they could walk), but Fly High Crew was less than one year old. Trey wasn't content with making up routines in the living room. He wanted to take his dancing to the next level.

The brothers founded the crew with Dani as the third member. Since then, a girl in Jax's class called Chantelle had joined. Dani had insisted on another girl to balance it out.

But in order to be taken seriously, the foursome needed to rehearse. And that's where the PE hall came in.

The crew shared the space with kids across year groups practising a load of different sports. At the moment, they were outnumbered by gymnasts, trampolinists and a huddle of kids practising karate.

But since sharing the space, Trey and Jax had got to know a handful of the other athletes. It turned out that a few of them had more in common than just their school. The first thing was that they lived in the Fernhill housing estate. And the second was that meeting every Tuesday was the highlight of their week.

Cameron, Layla and Madison were just as keen to perfect their skills as Trey, often staying late to get their drills correct. Cameron loved karate, Layla was committed to being a superstar gymnast, and Madison adored trampolining. Despite the odd clash, they all got on.

It wasn't perfect, but it would do. And even if it was annoying sharing the space with trampolines and gymnast beams, it was better than the alternative: no space at all.

Ms Tackle waved from the PE hall doors. "I'll be in my office marking if you need anything. Be careful! Don't break anything!"

"We always are, Miss!" Trey yelled back.

Jax bounced through the hall, narrowly

missing Cameron's foot connecting with his face.

"Yo, Cam!" Jax yelled. "Watch it with those roundhouse kicks!"

Cameron blushed, his rosy cheeks matching his red hair. "Sorry, Jax! I just got a bit carried away."

Looks were deceiving when it came to Cameron. He was tall, rangy, and he couldn't speak in class without blushing furiously. But his kicks looked like they could pack a punch. As Jax nearly found out.

Trey was keeping a close eye on Cameron. He knew that his mum had been ill for a little while, and needed a helping hand. The neighbours did the grown-up things: they dropped off food and helped with errands. But Trey made sure he had someone to talk to. It couldn't be easy for him.

"It's cool, Cameron," Trey said. "Jax needs

to watch where he's going!"

The brothers settled on the rubber mats that indicated their area. Trey wanted to make sure the boundaries were clear.

Chantelle was already there, warming up. Trey was sceptical about a newcomer joining Fly High Crew, especially since he was so tight with Jax and Dani. His brother was sometimes (OK, mostly) annoying but they understood each other. And Dani's mums had been friends with his mum and dad since for ever. She was like the older, sensible sister he'd never had. Or asked for.

Jax didn't know what to expect when Chantelle asked to join the crew. He only knew her as the quiet girl in his maths class. But as the weeks went by, she showed herself to be a real talent with a sharp sense of humour. It was like dancing brought out her shining personality.

The rest of the crew couldn't deny it: she was a quick learner and was very dedicated. In fact, Trey thought, she seemed a bit too dedicated.

"Trey, did you see my messages about today's routine?" Chantelle asked. "I thought we could try something new for the routine, like—"

Jax made a throat-slitting gesture with his hand and shook his head. Chantelle stopped talking mid-sentence.

"Er, I'll get back to you on that, Chantelle," Trey said, turning to refill his water bottle.

"What did I say?" Chantelle mumbled to Jax.

"Trey is dead fussy about his choreography," Jax said. "Once, Dani suggested a tiny change to the routine. It took weeks of negotiation! I'd leave it to him, if I were you."

"Speaking of Dani, any idea where she is?" Chantelle asked, pulling her hair into a high ponytail.

Trey bounced back to his crew with his water bottle. "You know what Dani's like. She rehearses when she feels like it."

"Hey, Trey! Hey, Jax!" Madison yelled from the trampoline, her blonde pigtails swinging with every bounce. She was the youngest regular at Tuesday rehearsals, and at one point, the shyest too. It was weeks before she said a word to anyone at rehearsal.

But Trey, Jax and Dani got to know her on the walks back to their housing estate after school. When Madison realized the crew weren't going to tease her about being born missing her left hand (it was no big deal to her, but a few nasty kids were mean on her first day at school until Trey told them to back off), she became a bit more chatty. Now, her confidence soared as high as her somersaults.

"How's it going, Mads?" Trey yelled back. "Slow down or you'll hit the roof!"

The dancers warmed up and assumed their positions in the cramped corner of the PE hall. Sandwiched between the trampolines and Cameron's karate crew wasn't ideal. But they would have to make it work.

"This space is tiny, man," Jax grumbled.

Trey clapped his brother on the back. "Don't sweat it. The talent show stage will be all the space we need."

"Oh, are you guys entering the talent show too?" Madison said. Then, she bounced upwards into a somersault and landed back on her feet. The whole thing was spectacular and took about 0.5 seconds. Even the spotters, two expert trampolinists from Year Eleven acting as coaches, looked impressed.

"Whoa," Trey muttered.

"Nice!" Cameron said. "But we're taking the talent show to the next level."

Before Trey could ask what that meant,

Cameron and the other karate athletes assembled. They wasted no time getting into their routine, performing a series of karate moves in exact synchronization. They looked powerful and impressive.

"Looking good! But what do you guys think of this?" Layla yelled from across the PE hall before executing a flawless handspring on the balance beam. Even her long black plait seemed to move in time, whipping through the air.

She was a Tuesday night rehearsal newbie, having moved to Park View High School just last term. She quickly became friends with the Fly High Crew when Dani invited her to sit with them for lunch.

Like Trey, she was a perfectionist. Trey never quite understood the appeal of gymnastics (all that jumping without music — what was the point?) but he still admired the skill involved.

Trey gulped. If they wanted any chance of

winning the Summer Talent Show, his crew had their work cut out.

He got the street dancers' attention with a firm whistle. "All right, squad! Let's take it from the top."

Jax rubbed his hands together, the most excited he'd been all day. "Let's do it!"

3

The hip-hop track blaring from Trey's phone came to an abrupt end.

"Those backflips are still looking a bit shaky," Trey said. "We need one more run-through and then you're free to go."

Trey ignored the groans coming from Jax and Chantelle. The street dancers looked on in envy as Madison and Cameron packed up their equipment and left.

"Oi, don't be like that! Don't you want to get it perfect?" Trey said. They'd never win first prize with that attitude.

"Bruv, can we get this over and done with?" Jax moaned, eager to get back home. His favourite conspiracy theory website, Area51. com, was bound to have a juicy story waiting for him.

"But we're so close to nailing this routine!" Trey said. "The hours we're putting in now will be worth it when we win the talent show."

"Can you tell that to my maths teacher? Because every minute I spend here is less time I have on my algebra homework," Chantelle said, sipping from a bottle of water.

"Nerd alert!" Jax said in a silly voice.

Chantelle punched him playfully on his arm. "Oi! Don't come to me next time you need to borrow a protractor."

"All right, let's call it a day. But please rehearse in your spare time. Once per week ain't enough!" Trey yelled over the sound of everyone packing up.

Trey and Jax were the last to leave, as usual.

"C'mon, man, I'm hungry," Jax said as Trey did a final sweep of the PE hall.

"You know what the deal is with Ms Tackle," Trey said. "We need to keep the space pristine if we want to keep rehearsing here."

No rehearsal space meant no Fly High Crew. Trey and Jax didn't know anyone with enough space to practise in their home. And the brothers were banned from living room backflips after the Smashed Vase Incident of 2019. Mum still wasn't over that one.

"Um, bro?" Jax said. "It's not Ms Tackle we need to worry about."

Trey dropped the rubber mat and joined his brother. Together, they watched through the glass-fronted PE hall doors as three adults walked towards the hall.

They'd recognize that bushy grey monobrow

anywhere.

It was Mr Crankshaw. And he was escorting two police officers down the hallway.

"What's going on? Do you think it's another Year Eleven prank gone wrong?" Jax asked.

The two police officers pushed through the double doors. Trey's heart beat a little faster.

"Can either of you explain why you're trespassing on private property?" one of the police officers demanded.

Jax's face screwed up. "What are you talking about? We're students!"

"You can speak to our PE teacher if you don't believe us," Trey said. "She's in the next room."

It was as though the brothers never spoke. "Take your things and leave," the other police officer said. "Consider this a warning."

Luckily, Ms Tackle burst in from the next room. "What on earth is going on here? Is someone hurt?"

The police officers turned, surprised to see Ms Tackle. "Do you know these young men? We received a call from the deputy head reporting two intruders in the PE hall."

Ms Tackle looked furious. "They're students, and they're using the PE hall for their after-school dance club."

Suddenly, Mr Crankshaw swung through the double doors. He must have been listening outside. "There must be a misunderstanding," he said smoothly. "I'm afraid I didn't recognize the boys outside of school uniform."

The police officers looked a little annoyed to Trey. "Right. In future, Sir, please do be more careful before making a call." Then they left as quickly as they'd arrived.

"Oh, Ms Tackle! Before you leave, we must have a chat about using the sports hall out of school hours. I have some health and safety concerns," Mr Crankshaw said. As they walked to her office, Mr C turned to Trey and Jax. "Your days in this rehearsal space are numbered, boys," he hissed, before scurrying away.

"You do realize he did that on purpose?" Jax said.

Trey nodded. "Yep."

"What would have happened if Ms Tackle didn't show up?" Jax asked. He looked worried.

Trey ignored the question. "Let's get going. I don't know about you, but I'm starving."

The brothers made their way out of the PE hall and bumped into Ms Tackle. As soon as they saw her come towards them with pursed lips, they knew she didn't have good news to share.

"We've left the hall just as you like it, Miss," Trey said quietly.

"I appreciate it, boys. But I'm afraid I have

bad news. Mr Crankshaw has some health and safety concerns about the PE hall being used by so many of you after hours," she said, tugging at the whistle around her neck. "I offered to supervise, but..."

"If it's too cramped, how about we get rid of the trampolines and gymnastics equipment? Surely Mr Stank — I mean, Mr Crankshaw would agree to that?" Trey said. He looked and sounded desperate.

Ms Tackle raised one eyebrow. "Well, I know they aren't part of your dance crew. But you do still have to share. And you never know, Trey. You might learn something from them!"

"It's just that this space is really important to us, Miss. Without the PE hall we have nowhere to practise. And if we don't practise, we'll never reach our full potential," Trey said.

And we'll never win first prize, he thought.

Jax couldn't help but admire his big bro. He knew exactly the right words to get a teacher's attention.

Ms Tackle nodded. "I'll do what I can. But, boys? I can't make any promises."

4

Trey and Jax stepped outside the PE hall. They were eager to get home and put this train wreck of a day behind them.

"Look! It's the ballet boys!" a familiar voice yelled.

Trey groaned. Did Logan have to start this mess again?

The rugby team captain and his boneheaded mates didn't let a week go by without tormenting the Fly High Crew. Funnily enough, Logan kept his distance when the martial arts group were practising.

"You lot wouldn't last one second in a rugby match!" Logan jeered. "Can't dance your way out of a scrum."

"Yeah? Well, it doesn't take much skill to chase a ball in the mud," Jax yelled back.

Logan narrowed his eyes. "What did you say to me?"

"You heard me!" Jax said. "Any idiot can throw or catch. It doesn't make you special. You're nothing but a snitch."

Logan's cheeks went red and he shoved his face in Jax's. "Shut up, pipsqueak!" he spluttered. "Or, I'll—"

"Or you'll what?" Trey said. He stood between Logan and Jax. "Hurt someone half your height? Real brave."

Logan and Trey were nose to nose. Unlike his little brother, Trey was one of the tallest boys in Year Eight. Ms Tackle was always on at him to join the basketball team.

Logan smirked but he did back away. "Come on, lads," he said to his mates. "Let's go before they backflip us to death."

They slinked away leaving Trey and Jax in the empty schoolyard.

"I could've handled Logan myself, y'know," Jax mumbled.

"I know," Trey said. "Anyway, we're gonna smash the Summer Talent Show and Logan will back off."

And that's when they saw it. A lightning-yellow blur.

"Yo! Did you see that?" Jax yelled.

They watched as the yellow blur raced across the school roof, darting over obstacles with the grace of a ballerina.

Only one person they knew could move like that.

Trey smirked. "So that's where Dani's

been hiding."

The brothers paused to watch their best friend in action. Her agile vault across the roof was something special.

"I swear that girl is part cheetah," Jax said.

Trey wished that Dani would use some of those skills for their street dance routine. She was one of the original Fly High Crew members, but lately she was spending more time outside. Her heart belonged to the concrete.

When Dani first described free-running to Trey, he was sceptical. Running around buildings with the odd backflip? It didn't sound anywhere near as fun, creative or cool as his beloved street dance.

Then he'd seen her in action around the tower block where they all lived. From his balcony, Trey watched as Dani hopped across the bike racks, balancing on each with the agility of a cat. From there, she launched herself to the bin shed roof with a single leap, and then (this bit was the pièce de résistance, as Mr Camembert would say in French class) she ran up the wall and backflipped neatly to her feet.

The girl had skills. Trey thought it then and he thought it now.

By the time Dani approached the edge of the school roof, the brothers were transfixed. How on earth was she gonna make it down? Her only option was to jump, but that would be one heck of a leap. At least twelve feet, Trey reckoned.

"No way is she gonna clear that!" Jax said.

"C'mon, let's get closer. She might need our help," Trey said. They both jogged towards the edge of the building.

Jax put his hands over his eyes and peeked through his fingers. "I can't watch, man!"

Dani stepped back to prepare for the ultimate

leap. She launched herself into the air and, at that precise moment, something really weird happened…

A green beam of light flashed down from the sky, causing Dani to stumble. Trey and Jax fell back, the shock of the green light knocking them off their feet.

The brothers watched in horror from where they had sprawled on the ground: Dani had lost her balance and begun plummeting to the ground, her arms and legs flailing in mid-air. She had to think fast! She tucked her knees, landed on her toes and immediately rolled over her shoulder before coming safely to a stop.

Curled into a ball, she looked like an armadillo in a hoodie. It wasn't quite the smooth landing she'd had in mind.

But it could have been a whole lot worse.

Trey and Jax got up and rushed over.

"Dani! Are you all right?" Trey asked,

helping her up.

She rose to her feet and dusted off her electric yellow hoodie. "I can handle a few tumbles, you know. How's my hair?" she asked, smoothing the frizzy brown curls framing her face.

"Forget your mop! Did you see that green light or what?!" Jax said, fizzing with excitement. "It came out of nowhere!"

Dani shrugged. "Must've been a helicopter or something. Or a plane on diversion." Trust Dani to come up with the dullest explanation ever. At thirteen, she was the oldest member of Fly High Crew and the most practical.

"That's such a grown-up answer," Jax said.

Trey chuckled. "Hey! Could be one of those top-secret government drones you're always banging on about?"

"Don't be stupid," Jax said. "Whoever heard of a drone shooting giant beams of green light?

The answer is obvious."

Dani raised one eyebrow. "Oh yeah?"

Jax took a deep breath. "It was an alien spaceship! I've seen the videos to prove it!"

Trey and Dani took one look at each other. Then they burst out laughing.

"That is jokes!" Dani said.

"Are you sure you didn't bump your head in rehearsal?" Trey asked.

"Whatever," Jax mumbled.

"So, why'd you miss rehearsal this time, Dani?" Trey asked.

Dani smiled like she was the cat with the cream. "Just felt like some fresh air."

"We might not have rehearsals for much longer, thanks to Stankshaw," Jax said.

"No way! What happened?" Dani asked.

"C'mon, it's getting dark. Let's make a move," Trey said. "I'll fill you in on the way home, Dani."

They began the short walk home. And with their backs to the school, the three friends didn't notice the hazy green glow that now surrounded the entire building.

5

Mum dumped dollops of tuna pasta on dinner plates. "I made your favourite, boys!"

Jax's stomach turned. Tinned fish was on his list of Top Three Worst Things to Exist alongside visits to the dentist and the sound of balloons rubbing together.

"Yes!" Trey cheered. He attacked his food with the ferocity of a starving tiger. Rehearsals always left him extra hungry.

"Cheers, Mum. I picked the right night to visit," Nate said.

"Dinner with all three of my sons!" Dad said, clapping his hands together. "What a blessing."

Between Dad's demanding job at the garage, Mum's shifts at the hospital and Nate's studies, dinners with the whole family were few and far between.

Jax and Trey's big brother was living on campus ages away while he studied for his physics degree. Visits from Nate were a rare treat now that he was well into his first year. If he came home at all, it was usually with a suitcase full of dirty laundry.

When Jax left home, he'd never eat tuna pasta ever again.

"I hate tuna pasta! Trey and Nate love it, but I can't stand it," Jax whined.

Mum turned from the stove. "Sorry, hun, but I'm too busy to make separate meals for everyone."

"Consider yourself lucky to have such abundance, Jax," Dad said. "I bet in Rome you wouldn't find such delicious tuna pasta!" He reached over to Mum and tickled her waist, then tipped a bottle of hot pepper sauce over his plate. Dad made it himself and it went on every meal.

Nate once dared Trey to eat a teaspoon of it. It took his tongue a week to recover.

"Enough with the lovey-dovey stuff, man! You'll put me off my food even more," Jax muttered.

Mum put her fork down. "I don't know what's got into you tonight, Jax."

"It's 'cause he hasn't had his Area51.com fix," Trey said, polishing his plate. "Can I have seconds?"

"Area51.com?" Dad asked. "Someone at the garage mentioned it today. Doesn't sound like a reputable news source to me."

"That's because it isn't," Nate said. "It's a conspiracy theory forum full of people who actually think aliens exist. Even though there's not a shred of scientific proof that—"

"Oh yeah? If you're such a brainiac, then how do you explain the bizarre weather appearing all over the world?" Jax interrupted. "I mean, there were hailstorms in the Amazon jungle! It has to be extra-terrestrial."

Nate peered at Jax over his glasses, like he was a teacher or something.

"I personally think climate change is to blame," Nate said. "But what do I know? I'm only a physics student."

Jax rolled his eyes. Could Nate be more annoying?

"Climate change doesn't explain that green light we saw at school today! Tell them, Trey."

"Jax, we've talked about this. It was a plane or a drone or something."

He shook his head. "No way. I've seen photos and videos and—"

"This is what I mean, Jax!" Trey yelled, spluttering half-chewed tuna pasta over the table. Jax wanted to gag. "You spend all your spare time on this bonkers website—"

"It's not bonkers," Jax interrupted.

"—And your head ain't in the game during rehearsals. I need you on Planet Earth, not flippin' Mars."

"This is quite concerning," Dad said, turning to Mum. "We gave Jax Nate's old laptop for homework, not so he can waste time looking for aliens."

"Don't worry about it, Dad," Nate said. "It's probably just a phase."

"I am right here, y'know?!" Jax yelled. He felt invisible.

"Jax! No shouting at the dinner table," Mum said. "And Trey, no phones at the dinner table either."

Trey was checking the Tuesday night rehearsal group chat again. He scrolled past the funny GIFs and Layla's panicked request for English homework help, but there was no sign of Dani. Usually, she was all over the group chat. Why was she so quiet?

Then, a message from Cameron caught his eye: *Mum's had a funny turn again :(*

Trey knew what that meant.

"Mum, is there any leftover tuna pasta? I'm gonna take some for Cameron. He just told me his mum's not very well," Trey said.

Mum's face fell. "Oh, poor Nina. Yes, be a love and take some food downstairs will you? And tell Nina that I'll be over tomorrow afternoon before my shift."

"Speaking of extra-terrestrials, has anyone beaten my high score on Alien Invasion yet?" Nate asked. As well as being a physics genius, he was unbeatable at the video game all three boys loved.

"I'm working on it!" Trey chuckled.

"Oh yeah?" Nate said, scraping the last forkful of tuna pasta into his mouth. "After dinner, you're on!"

"I'm going to see Cameron first," Trey said.

"Perfect," Mum said. "In the meantime, Nate, you can do your laundry. If you can figure out how to split an atom, you can figure out the washing machine."

No one else noticed when Jax left the table, went to his bedroom and softly clicked the door shut.

6

The next morning, the brothers set off for school. Trey's routine was the same every day: he got out of bed at exactly 7.45 a.m. and had showered, dressed and breakfasted by 8.19 a.m.

Jax's routine was also the same every day: he slept through the first three alarms and was eventually dragged out of bed by Mum or Trey around eight a.m. He somehow managed to shower, dress and swallow a piece of toast (he wasn't sure how, that part of the morning was always a blur) in record time.

Jax was especially tired this morning. He stayed up until late on his laptop, reading article after article about these bizarre weather patterns. And not just in the Amazon! Weird hailstorms were appearing in jungles and rainforests around the world.

He was convinced that Nate was wrong. Something fishy was definitely going on.

Trey and Jax met Dani by the cat bench on their housing estate (so called because it was colonized by a grumpy and sharp-clawed ginger cat called Butterscotch) and walked to school.

Well, the boys walked. Dani bounced off every available surface. She launched herself over dustbins, park benches and even the odd car bonnet. Dani probably did free running in her dreams, her long legs kicking under the duvet.

"You were quiet last night," Trey said to

Dani. "Stankshaw was getting torn to shreds in the group chat."

Jax laughed. "Yeah, you missed some killer GIFs!"

Trey had broken the news to the group chat last night. He decided it was better to be honest about the fate of their rehearsal space. Their support and banter cheered him up, even if it didn't solve the problem of where they'd rehearse.

No rehearsal space. No more Fly High Crew.

The thought left Trey with a queasy feeling in his stomach, like that time he'd had one packet of gummy bears too many. But this time sugary gelatine treats were the least of his problems. It was a certain monobrowed deputy head causing the trouble.

As they walked to school, Trey went into problem-solving mode. His eyes swept over the horizon, assessing everything in his neighbourhood for a potential rehearsal space.

The local park: too muddy.

The new gym: too posh.

The old church: too haunted (and it smelt like mothballs).

And those were the ones that had decent potential. The other buildings (mainly chicken shops, a cinema and the abandoned factory) were totally out of the question.

The trio arrived at school, the concrete yard filled with the chatter and laughter of other students. A rugby ball whistled past Jax's ear, narrowly missing his head.

"My bad!" Logan yelled. He had a nasty smirk on his face.

Something told Jax that he wasn't very sorry.

"Do you want me to take him out?" Dani said, her brown eyes flashing. "You know how quick I am. No one will ever find the evidence."

"It's nothing," Jax shrugged.

"Where are the teachers, anyway?" she asked. "I swear that Logan only strikes when none of them are watching."

"Looks like they have more important things to do," Trey said. He pointed to a queue of teachers waiting in line at a bright green vending machine, including Mr Crankshaw.

"Since when did we get a vending machine?" Dani asked.

"Cool! Maybe it sells crisps. Got a quid, Trey?" Jax asked.

"Don't get your hopes up, bro," Trey said. "I think it sells hot drinks."

They watched as the vending machine dispensed hot steaming coffee in little green cups. But as they got closer, they noticed something strange: the coffee was also green.

The funny colour didn't seem to stop the teachers. Unlimited free coffee just outside their classrooms? Christmas had come early for the staff of Park View High School. Most of the teachers here couldn't function without it.

Jax, Dani and Trey edged closer to the queue.

"It's about time they replaced the broken vending machine in the staff room," one teacher said to another. "But heaven knows why it's in the playground."

Jax stopped in his tracks. "Listen. Don't you think it's a bit strange that we saw the green flash last night. And now there's a massive green vending machine in the schoolyard? Giving away green coffee?!"

"Are the aliens to blame for that too?" Trey said laughing. Jax frowned at him.

"It's probably some publicity stunt for a coffee company," Dani said. "Remember that time when people dressed as giant potatoes handed out free crisps in town? I ate so many packets of salt & vinegar that my lips stung!"

Sensible as ever, Jax thought. Didn't Dani have any imagination?

The sharp sound of the bell blared through the air. Time for school.

"I've got Mr C first period," Jax moaned. "Wish me luck."

"Cheer up, Jax," Dani said brightly. "Maybe the free coffee will have put Stankshaw in a better mood?"

7

Jax bounced into classroom 4C and took his usual seat just behind Chantelle. When she wasn't being a nerd, Jax got on with her pretty well. She always had a spare pen whenever Jax forgot his pencil case (which was most days).

"Hey, Chantelle! Can I borrow a pen?" Jax said.

Chantelle rolled her eyes and rustled around in her pencil case. "Yes, but I'm only giving you a bog-standard biro. I'm still waiting for my scented gel pen back, you know."

The classroom door slammed open. "Quiet, Year Seven!" Mr Crankshaw growled. He dropped his jacket, laptop and coffee cup on the front desk.

After he took the register (he called Jax the wrong name again), Mr C announced the topic of that day's lesson: the Amazon rainforest.

Jax sat up straight. Thanks to his late-night news binge, this was a subject he knew loads about.

Mr Crankshaw wrote THE AMAZON on the whiteboard in big scrawling letters. "Now, Year Seven. Who can tell me a useful fact about the Amazon?" he asked, sipping on his coffee. "The rainforest, not the online retailer, before anyone gets smart."

Several hands shot up. As Crankshaw took down Amazon rainforest facts from the students, the whiteboard filled up.

Jax felt his phone vibrate inside his blazer

pocket. It was absolutely positively against school policy to have a mobile phone in lessons. If Stankshaw found out, he'd be toast. With Mr C facing the whiteboard, Jax quickly took his phone out and placed it on his lap.

He'd missed several updates from the Tuesday night rehearsal group chat, most of them ragging on Stankshaw (apart from Layla, who asked if anyone had seen her algebra textbook). Jax began typing: *I'm in his lesson right now! So boring!*

"You, boy!" Mr Crankshaw yelled, pointing to Jax. He immediately looked up from his phone. "An Amazon fact. Make it fast!" Mr C drained the cardboard cup of coffee in his hand, leaving a speck of green foam on his moustache.

Jax cast his mind back to the article he read last night. "Um, it's the biggest tropical rainforest in the world?"

Mr C's mouth puckered like a cat's bum. "Correct," he said quietly.

Jax wanted to punch the air with joy. He'd got the answer right and annoyed Crankshaw in the process. It was a double win.

Bzzzz. Jax's phone vibrated and flashed. Mr C looked up, like a hawk detecting its prey. If the buzzing sound didn't give him away then Jax's burning cheeks did the job.

A nasty smile crept on to Mr Crankshaw's face. "Is that a smartphone on your person, Jackson? Need I remind you that using smartphones in class is a suspendable offence. Especially if you're using them to search for the correct answer."

Mr C strode towards Jax's desk, trying to hide the glee on his face. He lived for getting students into trouble.

"I didn't cheat! I swear!"

Crankshaw towered over Jax's desk. "Prove

it. Unlock the phone and hand it over so I can see your search history."

Jax gulped. If he handed over the phone, Mr Crankshaw would see the group chat filled with messages tearing into their least favourite teacher. Everyone in their Tuesday night rehearsal club would be done for. There's no telling what heinous punishment Mr C would have in store for them.

Crankshaw's detentions were the stuff of legends at Park View High School. Rumour had it that Mr C wouldn't let Abdul Khan in Year Nine finish serving detention until he could recite every capital city in the world. Alphabetically. The poor kid still muttered "Beijing, Beirut, Belfast" to himself in the playground.

Mr Crankshaw held out his hand. "I haven't got all day, boy," he sneered.

Jax had no choice but to comply. He unlocked

his phone and placed it in Mr Crankshaw's hairy hand (even his wrists were bushy).

But the phone slid out of Mr Crankshaw's palm and landed on the floor with a clatter.

Jax looked up at Mr C. He seemed … different.

Mr Crankshaw stared into the distance with glassy eyes. Jax could have sworn they flashed green for a second.

Then, he heard what sounded like a car engine revving. But it was coming from Mr C's stomach. The old man clearly had serious digestive issues.

The revving sound didn't stop. In fact, it sounded like it was moving through Crankshaw's body. Now it seemed to come from Mr C's throat.

Suddenly, he spoke. "Activating. Scholar. Mode." His voice sounded tinny and metallic, like it was coming from a speaker rather than a person.

It was definitely coming from Crankshaw. So why didn't his lips move?

Mr Crankshaw began to walk backwards, taking small jerky steps like a rusty wind-up toy.

The entire class watched transfixed and whispered amongst one another. There was no denying it.

Something was very, very wrong.

Mr Crankshaw turned to face the whiteboard, picked up the marker pen and began writing.

"Look!" Chantelle whispered. "He's writing the same phrase over and over."

Jax squinted at the whiteboard. Chantelle was right. Mr Crankshaw was writing over their Amazon rainforest answers:

THE CAT SAT ON THE MAT. THE CAT SAT ON THE MAT. THE CAT SAT ON THE MAT.

Over and over again.

It was seriously weird.

Mr Crankshaw reached the edge of the whiteboard but didn't stop.

He carried on writing THE CAT SAT ON THE MAT, shuffling to the right with robotic movements. He wrote over the greyish-white walls. He wrote over the display of irrigation systems around the world. He even wrote over the windows.

"Are you all right, Sir?" Madison asked. She looked just as confused as everyone else.

Mr Crankshaw ignored her, continuing to write on the window and over the frames. It was like he was on teacher auto-pilot.

"Stankshaw's finally lost the plot!" One of the boys shouted from the back.

The entire classroom held their breath, waiting for Mr C to snap back and give that boy detention for life.

But Crankshaw never stopped writing.

THE CAT SAT ON THE MAT. THE CAT SAT ON THE MAT. THE CAT SAT ON THE MAT.

"Yo, Mr Monobrow! Does this mean we don't get any homework?" someone else stood up and yelled. The entire classroom collapsed into giggles.

Jax couldn't believe what he was seeing. Any second, he expected a film crew to burst in and reveal this was some prank.

But Jax knew that Mr C wasn't the practical joking type. His idea of a laugh was handing out detention slips.

As soon as the bell rang, Mr Crankshaw dropped the pen. He turned exactly ninety degrees to face his desk at the front of the classroom, picked up his things and took small jerky steps out of the classroom door.

Class 7B stopped laughing. This was getting creepy.

They walked out of the classroom in a daze. Did they really just witness the deputy head graffiti the entire classroom?

Jax lingered behind. Only he noticed that the green coffee cup on the desk was now empty.

8

By the time the three p.m. bell rang, the entire school was abuzz with what had happened. It was a warm afternoon, so Trey, Jax and a few other squad members walked home via their favourite chicken shop and sat in their favourite park. The trees were in full bloom and the smell of mown grass filled the air.

But the friends were too deep in conversation to appreciate the first real day of summer. It turned out that Mr Crankshaw wasn't the only teacher who had acted strangely that day.

Trey's maths teacher, Mrs Tally, scrawled the same algebra equation across the classroom door. And Layla's food tech class descended into chaos when Mr Blanche started mincing, dicing and chopping everything in sight. Her pencil case was ruined.

Madison chomped on her fries. "I bet it was a test. They're trying to see how we act without teacher supervision."

"I hate tests," Cameron groaned. "How on earth were we meant to pass that one? There was no exam paper, no essay question, no—"

"I'm telling you lot, it has something to do with that weird green vending machine," Jax interrupted. "That thing comes out of nowhere and then our coffee-addicted teachers start acting loopy? It's too much of a coincidence."

"You're missing the most important thing about this situation," Trey said, totally ignoring him. "Guys, don't you get it?"

They looked up at him with blank faces.

"Mr Crankshaw can't mess with our rehearsal space any more!" Trey yelled. "We might even be allowed to rehearse daily."

There'll be no stopping Fly High Crew from taking first place at the Summer Talent Show, he thought.

"Ooh! I really need to work on my drop tuck," Madison said.

While the friends chattered excitedly, Jax finished his hot wings in silence.

Green light. Green vending machine. Green coffee.

Jax tried to connect the dots in his mind, but he couldn't fill in the blanks.

This situation was like getting an itchy toe in the middle of a dance routine: irritating and impossible to satisfy.

"Yo, Trey. I'll see you at home," Jax said. He picked up the remains of his meal, left it beside an overflowing bin and walked away.

Jax arrived home to find Nate sitting on the sofa, having a cup of tea with Mum.

"Hello, sweetheart!" Mum said, pulling Jax in for a tight hug. She was in her hospital uniform.

"Leaving or coming back?" he asked. Mum's shifts were unpredictable these days.

"Leaving, I'm afraid. Dad called and said he's working very late tonight, so Nate is staying an extra night to watch you and Trey," Mum said.

"Hey, buddy!" Nate said in a high-pitched voice usually reserved for pets and toddlers.

Why was Nate acting like a distant uncle? There were only seven years between them.

"What's for dinner, Mum? I'm starving," Jax said. The hot wings were a distant memory, at least to his stomach.

"Nate's on dinner duty, my love," Mum

said, slipping on her black work shoes. "Don't stay up too late," she said, shutting the door behind her.

Jax turned to Nate. "If it's tuna pasta, I'm gonna switch."

His big bro laughed. "Nope! Tonight, my friend, we're having the Nate Special. In fact, I'm gonna get started now."

A little while later, Trey arrived home. He sniffed the air. "What's that smell?"

"It's the Nate Special," Jax said. He didn't take his eyes off the laptop screen. "He's cooking for us tonight."

Trey walked to the kitchen. "Nate, whatever you're making, can you do extra for our mate Cameron and his mum? I don't think they have much food at home right now."

Nate nodded. "Sure thing, buddy."

After an hour of Nate rattling around the kitchen and using what appeared to be every pot and pan they owned, he presented Jax and Trey with his triumph.

"I call them ... pizza bagels!" He laid plates stacked with several cheesy, tomato saucy bagels on Jax and Trey's laps. "They're my own invention, you know."

"Nice! Where's Cameron's?" Trey asked. "I'll take them down to his flat now."

"Wrapped in foil in the kitchen," Nate said.

"Cheers, bro. Back in a sec!" He got up and slipped on his trainers, picking up the pizza bagels wrapped in foil on his way out the front door.

Jax dived on to the pizza bagels like they were going to sprout doughy legs and run away.

"Be careful," Nate said. "They're really—"

"**AAAAAAGH!**" Jax screamed as molten cheese scorched his tongue.

"—hot," Nate finished. "Give them a few minutes to cool down."

By the time Trey got back from Cameron's, the pizza bagels were at an edible temperature. He sat on the sofa alongside Jax and tucked in.

"We're never going to finish all this food alone. Can I invite Dani over?" Trey asked. No one loved pizza like Dani. But since her mums Angie and Izzy decided to go on a health kick, their house was a cheddar-free zone. Apparently, oat cheese just isn't the same.

Also, Trey missed her. They had barely talked this morning, and she was nowhere to be seen after school.

Was Dani avoiding him?

"Fine by me," Nate yelled from the kitchen.

Trey fired off a quick message to Dani: *Nate made too much pizza. Wanna help us finish it?*

He saw from the blue ticks that she'd read his message immediately. Dani's flat was a couple of floors down, so she would be there any minute.

Nate sat on Dad's armchair and the brothers scoffed the now pleasantly warm pizza bagels. With their favourite football YouTube channel on in the background and making predictions about the FA Cup Final on Saturday, it almost felt like old times.

"So, what's the gossip at Park View?" Nate asked.

Jax dropped his bagel. "You wouldn't believe what happened to Stankshaw today!" Nate listened as Jax told him about the deputy head's rapid transformation.

"That's ... quite the story, Jax," Nate said. "Crankshaw was always on my back at school. Remember when he tried to have me suspended because of my canerows? I'd never seen Mum and Dad so angry."

"What was his face like when he saw your exam results?" Trey asked. "I would have paid anything to see it."

Nate passed all of his exams with flying colours, surpassing the expectations of their least favourite teacher. Trey and Jax were proud, even if having a brainiac big brother did make their lives trickier. He set the bar higher than Mount Everest.

He shrugged. "I don't care what Crankshaw thinks. You can't spend your life trying to prove ignorant people wrong."

Trey's phone buzzed. It was Dani.

Sorry, Trey. I can't. Busy tonight.

Jax eyed up the half-eaten pizza bagel on Trey's plate. "You gonna finish that, bro?"

"Nah," Trey said. "I've lost my appetite."

9

You'd think that the Powers That Be (aka, the head teacher, Mrs Upton) would shut down school after the deputy head vandalized his own classroom. At least for one measly day, Jax thought.

The next morning, he checked the school website constantly for an update. Maybe they'd announce an emergency teacher training day, or something.

But there was no such luck. It seemed like business as usual for Park View High School. It was as if the whole thing with Mr Crankshaw, Mrs Tally or Mr Blanche had never even happened. Apart from the faint permanent marker stain on the walls (Jax swung by to check between classes), classroom 4C was scrubbed clean.

At lunchtime, the friends sat in their usual corner of the canteen. Jax squeezed on to a bench with the rest of the crew. He unwrapped the foil over his sandwich, but a fishy stench stopped him dead in his tracks.

Tuna.

"Urghhhh, not again!" Jax yelled. He threw his sandwich on to the table.

"Wanna swap?" Dani asked with a hopeful smile. "I'd happily take your tuna fish if you take my broccoli wrap."

"Er, no thanks," Jax said. "I'll buy something instead. I think it's bangers and mash on Thursdays." He got up and joined the canteen queue for hot food.

"Yoink!" Trey swept Jax's uneaten sandwich on to his tray.

"Hey! I was gonna eat that," Dani said. She picked the broccoli out of her wrap.

Trey wolfed down his tuna sandwich. "You missed out on some epically cheesy pizza last night, Dani. Where were you?"

She tucked a stray brown curl behind her ear. "It's funny you should ask that. Because—"

"First tuna sarnies, now this!" Jax slammed his tray on the table.

They looked down at Jax's plate. The sausage and peas were frozen solid, the mash was still powdered and the whole plate was flooded with a lumpy onion-smelling brown goo.

"Everything's raw!" Madison said. She turned a little green. "Get that stuff away from me or I'll hurl."

Layla looked around the canteen. "I don't

think it's just you, Jax."

She was right. Staff and students alike looked down at their plates with confusion and disgust.

Now, the canteen staff of Park View High School weren't exactly churning out five-star cuisine. But their meals were usually at least edible.

This was a new low.

Dani pinched her nose. "Seriously, Jax, can you get that away from me? It looks and smells worse than my broccoli wrap."

"Guess I'm going hungry today," Jax muttered.

He took his tray and joined the long line of people queuing up for the food waste bin. He looked over at the dinner ladies. They were doling out scoops of powdered mash and frozen bangers, ignoring the disgusted looks and confused faces. One teacher was trying to reason with them, but they were ignored.

Jax gasped.

How did he not notice this the first time?

The glazed eyes. The synchronized mechanical movements. The ignoring of other people.

It was happening again.

And this time, Jax was certain of the cause. He dumped his tray on a nearby table and raced outside. Ignoring teachers who told him to slow down, he didn't stop running until he reached the schoolyard.

The green vending machine was still there. Teachers, staff members and even a couple of sixth form students were queuing up for green coffee.

In fact, the only member of staff in sight not queuing up was Ms Appleby, the school caretaker. She was trimming a hedge with a massive pair of shears.

Jax knew what he had to do. He didn't care

if he looked stupid.

It was the only way.

He took a deep breath and began to yell "DON'T DRINK THE—"

A hand covered his mouth. "Jax, what the heck are you playing at?" Trey hissed.

"Yeah, Jax, you can't go round shouting at teachers!" Dani said.

"But it's the green coffee! It's turning the teachers and the dinner ladies into … I dunno, like robots or something!"

Trey and Dani both looked a bit worried. Jax knew how it sounded. If he was in their shoes, he'd want evidence too.

Luckily, that's exactly what Jax had.

"Meet me at home straight after school," he said. "I'll explain everything."

10

Trey and Dani walked home together after school. They were going to be true to their word and give Jax the benefit of the doubt. Even if they did think he was a few sarnies short of a picnic.

Sure, Jax had always been a bit eccentric. Especially when it came to his conspiracy theories. But ever since they saw the green flash a few days ago, he was acting like a different person.

"He's obsessed, Dani. It's all he wants to

talk about at home," Trey said.

"You've got to admit, the last few days have been pretty bonkers," she said. "Did you hear about Ms Tackle?"

Trey nodded. Apparently, she did a one-woman bleep test in the PE hall. After two hours, she had to be escorted out by several teachers. According to Cameron, her feet were still running on the spot after she was bundled into a car and taken home.

"Yeah, it's been a wild week. And I haven't seen much of you."

She plastered a big fake smile on her face. The sort of smile Mum gave when Trey brought home half the squad for dinner unannounced.

"Well, I have exciting news... You know the Triple F's?" Dani asked.

"Course I do!"

Everyone in town knew about the Triple F's. The Fernhill Freerunner's Fleet were the best freerunners in the county. They even had a logo. And T-shirts! Trey could only dream of such things for Fly High Crew.

"Well, they asked if I wanted to join their crew," Dani said.

Now it was Trey's turn to wear a big fake smile. "That's sick, Dani! But don't you have to be over sixteen to join the Triple F's?"

"Usually, yes. But they're kind of making an exception for me. Apparently, I show great promise."

Wow. This was a huge deal. But all Trey could feel was betrayal.

"So, I guess this means you won't have time for Fly High Crew?" Trey said. *Or being part of the routine for the Summer Talent Show.*

"Um, I might! But the other Triple F's are super dedicated. They practise twice every week after school, plus Saturdays..."

"You do realize I'll have to redo the

routines?" Trey snapped. "If you're not part of the crew, everything changes!"

Dani looked surprised. "I didn't mean for that to happen. But this is an opportunity I can't turn down."

Trey got the message. Dani was going to be too busy with her new squad to mess around in the PE hall. *The Triple F's probably have a real practice space all to themselves*, Trey thought.

The two friends finished their walk home in silence.

Trey unlocked the door to their flat and entered, followed by Dani. The flat seemed quiet. Nate had gone home that morning and Mum must still be at work.

"I'm in here!" Jax yelled from his room.

Trey and Dani walked in. What they saw left them in silence for several seconds.

Every surface in Jax's room was covered with

post-it notes and scraps of paper: news articles, blog posts and scribbles in Jax's handwriting. A giant world atlas hung on the wall over his bed, held up by sticky tape.

"Jax, is this our old atlas?" Trey walked towards the colourful map and squinted.

"Yep. But now it's my Alien Hotspot Map! What do you think?"

When Trey and Jax were very little, the wall in their shared bedroom was decorated with this giant atlas. They marked the places special to them (Nigeria, where Dad was from, and New York City, which they both vowed to visit one day) with red circles. Trey could still see the faint markings.

Now the map was covered with green circles, some tiny and some taking up entire countries. Trey didn't have a clue what it meant.

Jax could see that Trey and Dani were

confused. He stood on his bed and used an old selfie stick as a pointer. "Let me explain. It all started a few weeks ago. According to Area51.com, strange weather patterns have been appearing all over the world. And it's the same everywhere: hailstorms that come out of nowhere. And what's weirder is that they're green," Jax said.

He thwacked the selfie stick across different points of the map highlighted with green circles. "First it was the Amazon rainforest. But they've also been sighted in Australia, Congo and Costa Rica," Jax continued.

Trey folded his arms. He didn't want to burst Jax's bubble, but at the same time… This was clearly a load of nonsense. "This is stupid, bro. You heard what Nate said the other day. This website isn't a real news site. Wise up!"

Jax frowned. "It's not just Area51.com! Newspapers, blogs and forums all around the world are saying the same thing." He pointed his stick at the print-outs plastered to his wall.

"If your theory is right, then this is colossal. So how come it's not headline news on every channel around the world?" Trey asked.

Jax hated when Trey put on his grown-up voice to ask boring questions. It was beyond irritating.

"That's the freaky bit! A few days after the hailstorm reports, the trail goes cold as ice. There's no more updates, no news stories, not even a tweet," Jax said.

"OK. But what does a hailstorm in South America have to do with our school?" Dani asked.

"The people reporting this weird weather also saw a bright green flash, just like we did. Precisely forty-eight hours before the green hailstorms," Jax said, trying to hold in his excitement.

Trey looked at the papers sellotaped to Jax's bedroom wall. If only he put this much effort into his homework or Fly High Crew rehearsals instead of a crackpot alien theory.

Jax turned to look at the world map. "I know it's connected to the green vending machine, the green coffee and the teachers going loopy. I just don't know how."

Dani was quiet for a second. "Well, if Jax's theory is right we will know once and for all any minute now," she said.

"What do you mean?" Trey asked. "Of course it's not right!"

"Fly High Crew rehearsal ended at 6.30 p.m. on Tuesday and we saw the flash not long after that, right? So, it's 5.39 p.m. on Thursday. All we need to do is wait for the green hailstorm," Dani said.

Trey snorted. "Hailstones in May?"

She turned to Jax. "And if we don't see any

green hailstones, do you promise to forget this and move on with your life?"

"Yes! Whatever you want!" Jax said. "Let's get going."

Trey looked puzzled. "Go where?"

"We need to go back to the source," Jax said. "Where we saw the green flash."

"What, the science block?" Trey said. "School's finished for the day. Why would you want to spend MORE time there?"

Jax crossed his arms. "Why can't you just listen to me, for once? No one in this house ever believes me!"

Dani sighed. "There's no harm in dropping by, Trey."

"Well," Trey sighed. "Seeing as it's so important to you ... we'd better get moving."

11

Jax raced to the school while Trey and Dani trailed behind. They cut through the park, and Trey couldn't help but notice everyone enjoying the warm evening. People were lounging on the grass, playing music and chatting together in small groups. One guy even had his top off.

Trey wiped his forehead, already damp with sweat from the jog back to school. It was simply too warm for hail.

"I'm gonna miss tonight's Triple F rehearsal," Dani grumbled. "All because Agent Jax has a theory to investigate."

Trey tried not to feel stung by the mention of his friend's new squad.

"Look, I know Jax. He'll get bored of this once he finds absolutely nothing special on the school grounds," Trey said.

"Then why are you going along with it?" Dani asked.

Trey stared at her like the answer was obvious. "Because he's my little brother."

Dani sighed. "Fine. On the bright side, Ma's making kale casserole tonight. Hopefully I'll get out of eating that."

Trey pretended to gag. "Remind me to never accept a dinner invitation to your place."

"Get a move on, slowcoaches!" Jax yelled. He was already at the school gate.

Dani looked nervous. "What happens if we get caught?" Although she was a daredevil free runner, Dani could be a right little goodie two-shoes sometimes.

Trey shrugged. "We make up an excuse, I guess. Say you've left French homework in your locker. Or you were walking your dog, and he wriggled through a gap in the gate."

She looked confused. "What dog?"

Trey chuckled. "You're really not good at making stuff up on the spot, are you?"

"Well, I don't make a habit of breaking and entering private property."

"Who said anything about breaking?" Jax asked. "We're using the special entrance."

Trey and Dani followed Jax to the back of the school, near the staff car park. There were a couple of cars still there, so they had to be extra careful to avoid being spotted. They slid their backs along the wall, inching towards the row of hedges separating Park View High School from the rest of the world.

"Nate told me about the special entrance

ages ago," Jax said. Then he dropped to his knees and disappeared behind a hedge.

After a few seconds, his head popped out. "You coming or what?"

Dani looked at Trey. "You owe me," she mouthed to him.

It was a tight squeeze, but the trio wormed their way into the school through a gap in the gate hidden by a hedge. They emerged in a shady corner of the schoolyard usually dominated by hostile Year Elevens.

"So that's why the older kids always hang out here," Dani said. "They're busting out every lunch break!"

"Shush! There's no time to waste. Let's go to the science block, where Dani nearly fell," Jax whispered.

"Hey! I didn't fall," Dani protested. "In fact, I executed a near-flawless tap landing."

They soon arrived at the science block,

inching along walls and ducking behind hedges to avoid being seen. Trey was tempted to hum the *Mission: Impossible* theme tune, but Jax didn't look like he was in the mood for a laugh. Apart from when they made it to level five of Alien Invasion, Trey had never seen him so focused.

"So ... what do we do now?" Trey said.

"We wait." Jax checked his phone. "It's nearly 6.30 p.m.! Any minute now..."

So, they waited.

"I can't see any hailstones, green or otherwise," Dani said after a few minutes. "Maybe we should call it a day and head home before it gets dark?"

Jax's shoulders slumped. Trey and Dani kind of felt sorry for him. "But ... my calculations! According to the hotspot map, it was meant to happen to—"

"WHO ARE YOU AND WHAT ARE

YOU DOING AT MY SCHOOL?"

Trey, Jax and Dani jumped into a ball and shielded their eyes from the ridiculously bright torch being shone into their faces.

"I-I-I left my dog in my locker!" Dani blurted out. Jax raised an eyebrow at her. She *really* needed to work on her excuses.

The bright torch disappeared. "Oh … you're students."

With a flashlight no longer burning their retinas to a crisp, they could see who was talking.

It was the school caretaker Ms Appleby.

They were so busted.

12

To their shock and surprise, the school caretaker didn't threaten to call the police, their parents or even escort them off the school grounds.

Ms Appleby seemed relieved. She switched off her torch (which was weird – it wasn't even dark yet) and put down her weapon. On closer inspection, Trey noticed it was a large spray bottle of weed killer.

"Dear, oh dear! You children did give me a fright," she said.

This was the closest any of the trio had been

to Ms Appleby. She was a plump, middle-aged woman with bright blue eyes and mouse-brown hair scraped back into a messy ponytail. No matter the weather, she always wore the same outfit: dark green wellies, dark blue overalls and a hooded parka. She looked like she worked on a farm in deepest Somerset, and not a suburban secondary school that was more concrete than grass.

Ms Appleby had been the caretaker for as long as the school had existed, but she mainly kept to herself. She didn't eat lunch with the staff in the canteen or volunteer to chaperone at the school disco.

In fact, this was the first time any of them had heard her speak. She had a nice West Country accent. It reminded Trey of the time his family took a seaside trip to Cornwall last summer.

"Wait. You're not angry?" Dani asked.

"I have much bigger frankfurters to fry, little one," Ms Appleby said mysteriously. "Something strange is afoot."

"It's to do with the green vending machine, right? And the teachers going loopy?" Jax asked.

Ms Appleby narrowed her eyes. "How much do you know?"

"I know that every grown-up who drank that green coffee lost the plot straight after," Jax said. "I saw Mr Crankshaw transform with my own eyes!"

"Never trust green coffee, is what I say. But no one listened to old Appleby," she muttered.

"No one listened to me, either!" Jax said.

Before Trey or Dani could stop him, he launched into a blow-by-blow account of the past forty-eight hours. He told Ms Appleby about the green flash, the green hailstorms around the world, and how he believed it was all connected.

"…and that's why we're here! Because the green hailstorm is due to arrive any second now," Jax said.

"Sorry, Miss. My little bro has a wild imagination," Trey said.

"He spends way too much time on these weird conspiracy theory websites," Dani said.

Jax felt his cheeks grow hot. "Hey! They're not weird," he protested.

But Ms Appleby didn't dismiss anything Jax had to say. She just nodded.

Suddenly, a clacking sound filled the air. It was the sound of glass beads tapping, or…

"HAIL!" Jax yelled.

Tiny hard pellets rained down from the sky. Trey felt them bounce off his arms and on to the ground, where they melted on the concrete and into the grass.

Jax dropped to his knees. "Look, they're

green! I was right!"

Trey squinted at the ground, but the hailstones melted too quickly for him to notice any colour.

Dani looked up. "It's too warm for hail. And it's not even that cloudy!"

Ms Appleby slapped her forehead. "My babies! The hailstones will ruin 'em!" She jogged away, the chain of keys on her utility belt rattling. The three friends followed.

As soon as they reached the caretaker's shed, Ms Appleby turned to the children. "I'm afraid I'll have to swear you to secrecy. What lies inside this shed is a serious infraction of every Park View High School regulation. That Crankshaw would have my guts for garters if he knew the truth."

Jax nodded furiously. "Your secret's safe with us, Miss!"

Trey and Dani nodded too. Curiosity was

getting the better of them.

Ms Appleby led them into the shed and switched on the light. So far, so normal. It was full of ladders, old tins of paint and sacks of soil. Dani pinched her nose. It did smell a bit ... manure-ish.

They carefully wound their way through the shed stacked with boxes and overflowing shelves.

"Is her secret that this shed is a health and safety nightmare?" Dani whispered to Trey.

When they reached the back wall of the shed, Trey began to wonder if Ms Appleby had accidentally knocked over a bottle of paint thinner and inhaled the fumes. Where was she taking them?

She unclipped the chain of keys on her utility belt, held them up to her ear, and gave them a good shake. Trey and Dani backed away slightly.

"There's a method to my madness, children. You see, the key to this door has a slightly different sound than the others," Ms Appleby said.

"What door?" Dani asked. They were facing a blank wall.

Ms Appleby stamped her feet. "This one!" She kicked off a sheet of blue tarpaulin to reveal a trapdoor.

"This is so cool!" Jax said.

"Mind yourself," Ms Appleby said. She crouched down and placed the key in the lock. The hinges made a creepy, creaky sound as the wooden door flipped open. The three friends watched as Ms Appleby crawled down into the darkness below.

Using their phones as torches, Trey, Jax and Dani stepped into the tunnel and crawled through on their hands and knees.

"Don't mind the mice! They only take the

odd nibble," Ms Appleby yelled ahead of them.

The trio crawled faster.

A few seconds-that-felt-like-hours later, they emerged back into the evening sunlight on the other side.

Trey looked around. "Where are we?" It didn't look like any part of the school grounds he'd ever seen.

They were in a patch the size of a small classroom. It was bordered on three edges by overgrown bushes and on one edge by the high wall of Ms Appleby's shed. Neat rows of soil and big green leaves covered the ground.

"Oh! It's an allotment," Dani said. "My mums use theirs to grow onions."

Ms Appleby beamed. "You've hit the nail on the bread, my girl. This allotment is my pride and joy."

"This is your big secret?" Jax asked, clearly deflated. He expected something way cooler than a pile of dirt and leaves. Maybe wreckage from a spaceship or dust from a fallen asteroid.

Not vegetables. And green vegetables at that. They were objectively the very worst kind.

"Why would Mr Crankshaw be mad about this?" Trey asked.

"Ah, let's just say that I've used some … unconventional methods to fertilize my babies. But if the students want to waste perfectly good gravy, I'll find a use for it," Ms Appleby said.

"What are you growing?" Dani asked. "Peas? Carrots? Lettuce?"

"Well, I was eating my tea one day and I says to myself, 'Appleby, what if someone combined your two favourite foods in the whole world?'"

"Like a pizza–burger!" Jax said.

Trey's eyes lit up. "Or a tuna pasta pie!"

Ms Appleby nodded. "But I went one step further. Behold, the spabbage!" she yelled, whipping over a giant green leaf with the flair of a magician. "It's my own invention: a spinach and cabbage hybrid. All the yummy flavour of spinach with the scrumptious fragrance of cabbage."

Even Jax gave Ms Appleby a funny look. "That's, like, the worst things about both."

"Whoa," Dani said. "They're huge!"

"And so … green," Jax said. "Bet you could see them from outer space."

Each spabbage was roughly ten times the size of the average cauliflower, with dark green leaves the size of pillowcases.

"Aren't they beauties? We'll be harvesting any day now. And don't worry, I'll be sure to save you all a spabbage of your own!" She winked.

"Er, thanks," Trey said.

Jax pointed to a spabbage by his feet. "Hey, Ms Appleby? I think you should take a look at this."

The caretaker flicked on her torch and shone it on the ground. "No! Not my babies!" she cried.

The spabbage was transforming before their very eyes. The deep green colour drained from the mutant vegetable, leaving it grey and withered.

"Look, it's spreading!" Jax yelled. Sure enough, the other spabbages were turning grey and shrinking. He whipped out his phone and filmed the whole thing.

Ms Appleby pulled out a hosepipe and

showered the spabbages with water. But it was no use. In a matter of minutes, all of the spabbages were reduced to dry grey lumps.

The three friends didn't know much about gardening. But they did know that what they saw was far from normal.

"I'm sorry about your weird veg, Miss," Jax muttered. "Do you reckon it has something to do with—"

Trey shushed his brother. "Not now, Jax."

Ms Appleby sobbed. "In all my years of gardening, I've never seen a thing like this!"

The three friends couldn't help but feel terrible for her. She looked heartbroken. But it was getting dark (and chilly).

"Miss, we should be going home," Trey said.

The three friends waved goodbye to a forlorn Ms Appleby and slipped down the tunnel.

"Mum's gonna flip when she sees our

uniforms," Trey said as they trudged home. Thanks to their trip through Ms Appleby's trap door and the secret entrance behind the hedge, their grey school trousers were filthy.

Dani picked up the pace. "Can we walk quicker? I'm not supposed to be out after dark."

They walked down the main road. "Hey, watch out!" Dani yelled. She pulled Trey back as an unmarked van sped through a red light.

He was clearly shaken. "Thanks, Dani," he muttered. "Guess my mind was elsewhere."

The van drove down a narrow street and stopped at the solid gates of a red brick building. It was the old factory.

"Whoever's driving that van can't be from around here," Dani said. "Otherwise, they'd know that the factory has been abandoned for—"

She stopped talking. To her surprise, the heavy iron gates shuddered open. They left just enough space for the van to creep through.

"Huh. Weird," Trey said.

This was strange. But given what they'd just seen at school, it was quickly forgotten. Between the green hailstones and discovering Ms Appleby's franken-veg allotment, this was shaping up to be one of Jax's stranger Thursday evenings.

He had a feeling that the spabbages turning grey was linked to the green hailstones. But how? If he was going to figure it out, more research would be needed.

It was going to be a long night.

13

The next morning, Trey went to drag Jax out of bed at 8.05 a.m. "Time to wake up, bro!" he said cheerfully (yes, Trey was a morning person) as he threw back the duvet.

But Jax wasn't there.

Instead, Trey found Jax at the breakfast table. He was fully dressed and totally conscious. Jax looked up from his toast. "I wondered when you'd finally get out of bed."

Mum burst into the kitchen. "Morning, boys." Then even she did a double take. "Jax!

You look so … awake."

"What can I say? We've got a big day at school," Jax said.

Last night's misadventures with Ms Appleby came flooding back. Trey hadn't dreamed about the secret allotment or the spabbages, had he?

But the grazes on Trey's elbows from crawling into the tunnel were very real. Last night definitely wasn't a cheese-induced fever dream. It has actually happened.

"I'll be home a bit later than usual tonight, sweethearts," Mum said. She rushed around the kitchen, tossing her phone, keys and purse into her cavernous handbag.

"Another double shift?" Trey asked.

"Yes. Several of my colleagues just didn't bother to show up, apparently. I've never known anything like it," Mum muttered.

Jax's eyes lit up. He took out a notepad from his blazer pocket and scribbled something down.

"And don't forget Dad's working late every night this week," Mum added.

"But he'll definitely be home on Saturday, right? It's the FA Cup Final!" Trey said. Watching their first FA Cup Final without Nate was weird enough. Dad *had* to be there.

Mum snorted. "Now *that* your father won't miss." She gave the two brothers a kiss goodbye, instructed Trey on how to heat up the leftovers for dinner, and raced out the door for work.

"C'mon, Trey. We need to leave!" Jax said.

Trey screwed up his face. "OK, what is up with you? First, you're up early for school. And now you want to arrive early?"

"If I'm gonna get to the bottom of this mystery, I need to have my ears to the ground. Look out for anything strange, OK?" Jax asked.

Little did they both know that this was about to be the strangest Friday in Park View High School history.

★

The walk to school started off pretty normal. Jax was banging on about aliens, Dani couldn't stop talking about the Triple F's, and Trey was getting pretty cheesed off with both of them. The Summer Talent Show was only a few weeks away and they had nothing close to a proper routine. But Jax and Dani didn't seem to care.

Jax's French teacher seemed a bit more stressed than usual. Apparently an unusually high number of teachers weren't available. Something about an emergency teacher training day.

Yeah right, Jax thought.

The remaining teachers had to mind several classes at once. Poor Mr Camembert was in a right state, ducking in and out of three classrooms throughout the lesson. It's no wonder that the frazzled teachers were more desperate than ever for free coffee at the morning break.

And that's when everything started to go wrong. Every teacher on the grounds had a cup of free green coffee in their hands. By the time third period ended, the weirdness was undeniable.

The teachers were on the rampage.

When Trey, Jax and the rest of their friends made it outside for their lunch break, the school was like a war zone. They met in their favourite corner of the schoolyard. All were desperate to share stories about how their teachers had gone into meltdown.

"Miss Stipple couldn't stop painting in art class!" Madison reported breathlessly. "She covered Jill Johnson's blazer with yellow polka dots."

"That's nothing. You should have seen Mr Patatas!" Cameron interrupted. "He conjugated every Spanish verb from memory speaking at, like, a million miles per hour. I swear that smoke came out of his ears!"

"Don't even think about going to the canteen," Chantelle said. "The dinner ladies were lobbing jacket potatoes at anyone who came close to the hot food section. I managed to grab a ham and cheese sandwich and then ran for it!"

Trey looked over at Jax, waiting for him to come out with something like "aliens" or "spabbages" or "don't trust the green vending machine". Instead, he was too busy writing in his little notepad.

"Guys, I have an idea," Trey said. "If the teachers are acting up, let's spend the rest of this afternoon rehearsing. Think about it! I bet we'll have the PE hall to ourselves."

"Trey, I narrowly missed being knocked-out by a baked potato. Dancing is the last thing on my mind," Chantelle said.

"Why don't we just bunk off?" Layla asked. "It's the perfect weather for it."

"Because Crankshaw doesn't need an excuse to boot any of us out of school. I bet he has beady-eyed informers everywhere," Dani muttered.

"Oh, gosh. I have chemistry next. What if Mr Litmus sets the class on fire with Bunsen burners?!" Cameron said, panicking.

"I'm not waiting to see which teacher destroys a classroom first," Dani said. "Trey's right: let's head to the PE hall until home time. We'll be safe there."

14

Chantelle was right: there was no way Fly High Crew could rehearse in these conditions. They didn't have their PE kit, firstly. And secondly? They could hear the crashes, bangs and wallops of their school being torn apart by the teachers of Park View High. It was somewhat distracting.

Trey and his friends sat on a pile of rubber mats in the PE hall, waiting until it was safe for them to leave.

Layla fiddled with her hair. "What do you

think's going on? I've never seen any teacher act like this before."

Jax stood up. "I think I know what's going on. This is going to sound weird, but just let me finish, yeah?"

For several minutes, the squad listened patiently as Jax filled them in. And he didn't hold back any detail. The green flash they saw after rehearsal. The green vending machine dispensing free green coffee turning up the next morning. The teachers and dinner ladies acting like robots. The green hailstorm last night (but not the spabbages, as Jax remembered his promise to Ms Appleby).

To Trey's shock, the rest of the squad didn't laugh.

They were transfixed.

"I saw the green hail last night, too!" Madison piped up. "Dad and I had to rush out and get the laundry in before it got wet.

But the hail bounced off the clothes and on to the ground. It melted before I could get a photo."

"We get it, Jax," Trey said. "Things have been a little strange these past few days. But—"

"Now that you mention it, my dad was acting kind of weird last night," Layla interrupted. "He came back from the office and wouldn't stop babbling about spreadsheets. Like, all night. Mum had to sleep with earplugs in."

"And my mum definitely wasn't herself," Cameron said. "She used to be a receptionist, before she got sick. And this morning she wouldn't stop answering these made-up phone calls at the kitchen table. When I left for school, she was telling a bunch of bananas to 'hold, please'."

Jax nodded and took notes in his little notepad.

"So, what do you think it all means, Jax?"

Chantelle asked.

He sighed. "I don't know yet. I've noticed similar patterns in other places around the world. According to the forums, the pattern is always the same: green flash followed by green hail forty-eight hours later. But then the updates stop."

"Further proof that it's all someone's idea of a joke, maybe?" Dani said.

Jax shook his head. "Dani, have you seen what's going on out there? Every grown-up in the entire school is behaving like a robot having a meltdown. They just do the same thing on repeat … but, really badly."

An almighty BANG interrupted their conversation. Something pounded on the PE hall door. The friends huddled into a corner.

"Stu. Dents. Must. Oh. Bay." The mechanical-sounding voice blared through the door. It was so eerie.

"Who the heck is Stu Dents?" Madison whispered.

"They're saying 'students must obey'," Dani realized. "They're talking to us!"

Jax broke away from the huddle and peered through the glass-fronted doors. He gasped.

A green-eyed Mr Crankshaw stood at the door, his gaze bright as a laser beam. And he had company.

"It's Stankshaw!" Jax whispered. "With loads of other teachers. Their eyes are glowing green and they're trying to get in!"

Thankfully, Dani had had the bright idea of bolting the door when they entered the PE hall. But the door was bulging inwards with the force of a dozen robot teachers pushing against it. It wasn't going to hold for much longer.

Jax ran towards the glass doors leading outside. He slapped the glass and tugged at the handle but it was no use. "This one's locked!" he yelled.

Trey pointed to a door at the opposite end of the hall. "Let's try Ms Tackle's office! We can climb out of the windows."

He and the crew ran towards the office door and pushed it open. It opened a crack, then jammed. Something was lodged against the door to stop it from opening fully.

"What's wrong?" Chantelle asked.

"Hurry!" Layla yelled.

Suddenly, Logan appeared through the glass panel in the door.

"Oi, Logan! The door's stuck!" Trey yelled.

"It is? Someone should sort that out for you," he sneered.

"Why would you lock us in?!" Jax yelled. "Those teachers are out for blood!"

"Serves you right for being such a show-off!" Logan spat. Then he ran through Ms Tackle's office and climbed out of the open window into the playground. He was gone.

"OK. Now we need a Plan B," Dani said, trying to keep calm.

"How do we keep them out?" Jax said, eyes wide with fear. Normal Crankshaw was scary enough.

But Robot Crankshaw? He was pants-wettingly terrifying.

"The vaulting horse! Over there," Layla pointed to the tall cushioned box she used for gymnastics. It was the perfect height for blocking the door, and it looked sturdy too. If the entire squad hurried, they could block the door before the bolt snapped. Maybe.

"Let's move!" Trey yelled.

The crew ran across the hall to the vaulting horse. But it was way too light. It skidded on its wheels and thumped against the bolted door.

"This thing couldn't keep out a kitten!" Jax said.

Trey nodded towards the supply cupboard. "Then we add reinforcements."

The friends formed a line from the supply cupboard to the PE hall doors. Moving with the swiftness of an army, they stacked a gym mat trolley with anything remotely heavy: bags of basketballs, poles and cricket bats were piled on. They rolled the groaning trolley to the door and added a couple of plank benches to the load for good measure.

Out of all the ways Trey expected that Friday afternoon to end, it wasn't being barricaded in the PE hall with marauding teachers on the loose. He was meant to be in Double English, where the biggest risk was a papercut from an old textbook.

But thanks to their quick-thinking, they were safe from the clutches of green-eyed-robot Crankshaw. Their PE barricade had bought them a bit more time.

There was just one problem.

"Um, gang?" Dani asked. "How the heck are we going to get out?"

Dani was right. They were trapped.

15

Suddenly, a loud slapping sound came from the window. The squad spun around to see Ms Appleby's face pressed against the large glass doors leading outside.

"Oh gosh, not another one!" Madison yelled.

"Nah, Ms Appleby's cool," Jax said, running towards the door. "Look! Her eyes aren't green and she's not moving like a rusty robot."

"Yeah, Ms Appleby won't go near that nasty green coffee," Dani said.

"We're trapped, Miss! The teachers are on the

other side," Jax yelled. He tugged at the door handle but it was no use. They were locked in from that side, too.

"I can't unlock the door from outside!" Ms Appleby yelled. Her ponytail was even messier than usual and her face was smeared with mud. But with a hammer, torch and several cans of spray paint hanging from her utility belt, Ms Appleby looked like she could take on anything.

"Stand well back, children!" Ms Appleby took a running high-kick that even had Cameron impressed and launched herself on to the glass door.

But she collapsed into a heap. The glass didn't have so much as a scratch.

The crew fell silent. "Well. That was awkward," Dani muttered.

Ms Appleby stood up slowly, dusting herself off. "Damn that double glazing!" she yelled.

At that moment, there was a cracking sound

coming from the other side of the PE hall. It was the door. The bolt and barricade wouldn't hold much longer.

"Miss! Is there any other way we can escape this hall?" Trey pleaded.

"Of course! Children, listen very carefully," Ms Appleby said. "You see that supply cupboard? At the very back there's a hidden entrance to the PE Block staircase."

Dani shook her head. "Miss, you've made a mistake. The staircase is on the other side of the building."

"You listen to me, girly! I know this school like the back of my ham," Ms Appleby said.

"Did she mean to say 'hand'?" Chantelle whispered.

"She does that a lot. You get used to it," Jax whispered back.

"Run to the supply cupboard and tap the back wall for the door. Go through that door and down the PE Block stairs, and you'll see the fire exit leading to the staff car park. You'll be safe there," Ms Appleby said.

The friends didn't waste any time in obeying. They rushed to the supply cupboard and set to work finding this door.

"Stu. Dents. Must. Oh. Bay." The mechanical chorus grew louder. It seemed like every teacher in the school was on the other side of that door.

Jax shuddered to think what they'd do if the bolt snapped.

Finally, they found the secret door.

"It's here!" Dani yelled. She tugged at the doorknob and the door shook. But it didn't open.

Trey pushed her out of the way. "Let me try," he said and pulled at the doorknob with all his might.

Dani folded her arms. "It's locked, Trey. You can pull all you want! Without a key it's hopeless."

The keys. Jax sprinted from the supply cupboard to the window. "Miss, the door's locked! Do you have a key?"

Ms Appleby nodded and shook the giant chain of keys on her utility belt. "I have the keys. But it's getting them to you that's the problem!"

Jax turned to face the door. The slow, rhythmic pounding was wearing down the bolt.

There was no way it would hold much longer.

Then, Ms Appleby did the last thing Jax ever expected. She ran away.

"What did Ms Appleby say, Jax?" Chantelle asked. The tremor in her voice betrayed her fear.

"She … um…" Jax began.

Before he could finish, the secret supply cupboard door swung open. It flooded the dark cupboard with light.

There, in the doorway, stood Ms Appleby.

"Quick, children. There's no time to lose!"

Ms Appleby had no idea how right she was. At that exact moment, the bolt snapped and flew across the PE hall. It landed on the ground with a crash.

"Stu. Dents. Must. Oh. Bay." The teachers sounded clearer than ever. They were in the hall. It was only a matter of seconds before they looked in the supply cupboard.

The squad dropped to the floor to avoid being seen, then crawled on their hands and knees through the secret door in single file.

Jax was last in line. His heart pounded as he slowly shuffled across the floor.

Then he saw it. Robo-Crankshaw's head popped through the door. His eyes were greener than ever, the light from it casting an eerie glow over the cupboard.

His gaze landed on Jax. A mechanical churning sound came from his throat. He was trying to speak.

Robo-Crankshaw jerked his arm and pointed at Jax's feet. "No. Lei. Sure. Shoes. On. School. Grounds!" He angled his body towards the door and moved slowly towards Jax with his arms outstretched. Jax had never been so scared.

Ms Appleby leaped over Jax and burst into the PE hall. "Run for your lives, little ones!" Ms Appleby yelled. She aimed two bottles of weed killer in Robot Crankshaw's face and sprayed.

Suddenly, Robo-Crankshaw staggered back in pain. But Jax could hear the other robo-teachers gaining ground. And Ms Appleby was already out of weed killer.

"What are you waiting for, man?!" Trey whispered from the other side of the door.

"But what about Ms Appleby?!" Jax asked frantically.

"She can clearly look after herself. Let's

move!" Trey yelled.

Jax hoped he was right. The squad burst out of the fire exit, ran through the staff car park and out of the school gates.

They didn't stop running until they got home.

16

"Here comes the popcorn!" Dad said. "Half salty and half toffee, just as you like it." He placed a giant bowl of fresh popcorn on the sofa between Trey and Jax.

But the brothers weren't exactly in the mood for snacks. Which was weird, because Trey and Jax never turned down Dad's signature salty-toffee popcorn. Getting chased by robo-teachers and escaping by the skin of your teeth kind of ruined the appetite.

The events of the day before were still on

their minds. Once Mum came home from work, Trey and Jax told her everything that happened at school.

Mum frowned. "You're both far too old for tall tales," she said. "Don't be so daft!"

Jax was about to protest but Trey stopped him. Mum would only think they were lying and they'd get into more trouble.

Now it was Saturday and the FA Cup Final was due to start any minute. Usually, the boys would be excited to watch the football match of the year with Dad. Especially as he'd been so busy at work lately. But Jax couldn't forget Robo-Crankshaw's bright green gaze. He'd barely slept last night. Every time he closed his eyes, those lizard green eyes tormented him in his sleep.

"You boys are quiet today," Dad said. "Not a peep out of either of you, eh?"

"Tired, I guess. Busy week at school," Trey muttered.

Dad laughed like it was the funniest thing he'd heard in days. "Wait until you get a job, my boy. Then you'll know the meaning of busy."

The first half of the match went by in a blur. Jax and Trey ignored the TV and the humungous bowl of popcorn. They were much more interested in the group chat:

CAMERON: My mum is still answering phone calls from the fruit bowl ... it's so odd.

LAYLA: Mum's taken me and my little sisters to Aunty Nadia's house. Dad wouldn't stop talking about spreadsheets for two whole days. Getting weird now.

The rest of the crew tried telling their parents and carers about their lucky escape from the school, and the grown-ups reacted in much the same way: they either laughed, told them not to make up stories, or ignored them altogether.

"GOOOAAALLLLLLL!" Dad yelled,

leaping up from his chair.

The sudden shout made both boys jump. Their nerves were still on edge.

"You missed it! Too glued to your phones," Dad tutted.

The front door opened and closed. "Can I get a hand with the shopping?" Mum yelled. "And I've got a special treat for your father…"

"Perfect! It's half time anyway," Dad said. He left Trey and Jax in the living room to help Mum in the kitchen.

The boys scrolled through the group chat, reassuring their friends that everything would be all right. Even if they didn't quite believe it themselves.

"Poor Cam and Layla," Trey said.

"I can't stop thinking about Ms Appleby," Jax said. "What if she didn't get away in time?"

But Trey didn't answer. He stood up and walked towards the TV. "Jax? Tell me this is all in my head."

Jax looked up and realized what Trey was talking about.

The football pitch on the TV was changing colour.

The grass at the edge of the pitch slowly transformed from a lush green to a dull grey. The grey colour moved towards the centre of the pitch, like water swirling down a drain. It was as though something underneath the pitch was sucking the grass dry, leaving dusty grey remains.

"Just like the spabbages!" Jax said.

Trey nodded. It was exactly like the spabbages, just on a much bigger scale.

"Where are the players? Why isn't anyone doing anything?" Jax asked.

"Mum and Dad have got to see this," Trey muttered. He ran into the kitchen followed by his little brother.

"Come and see this! The pitch at Wembley Stadium … it's changed colour!" Trey yelled.

Mum and Dad had their backs turned to the boys. They were looking at something out of the kitchen window.

"Mum? Dad?" Jax asked tentatively.

Their parents didn't budge. It was like talking to a brick wall.

Jax's stomach felt weird. Weirder than the time he rode the Scorpion rollercoaster after eating his body weight in chips.

For a second, everything was deathly quiet. Then Trey and Jax heard something. A mechanical creaking sound. It was coming from their parents.

Inside their parents.

Jax stepped closer. "Are you guys all right?"

"Hey, Jax. Don't get any closer," Trey whispered.

Suddenly, Mum and Dad started to move.

They jerked their bodies round to face the boys, both clutching green coffee cups in their hands.

They both spoke at the same time. "Activating. Parent. Mode."

Trey and Jax gasped. They didn't stay long enough to see the green flash in their eyes.

They ran.

17

Trey and Jax didn't have to run far before they saw it. The green vending machine was slap bang in the centre of the housing estate's courtyard.

"Mum must have picked up free coffee for her and Dad after she did the shopping," Trey said.

Jax nodded. Grown-ups love nothing more than a freebie, and their parents were no exception.

Usually, their neighbours would be out and

about on a sunny Saturday afternoon. But there was no one around. It was eerily quiet.

"We need to warn the rest of our crew," Jax said. He typed a frantic message to the group chat urging them to make sure their parents didn't drink the free green coffee.

"But what about Dani? She's at Triple F's practice! We can't risk letting her come home to robo-mums," Trey said. He patted his pocket and realized that, luckily, his phone was there and not at home.

The brothers raced across town to the Fernhill Freerunning Academy. Despite the fact that this was the weirdest weekend of Trey's life, he still felt a pang of jealousy that the Triple F's had a proper practice space and Fly High Crew didn't. He couldn't imagine setting foot in the PE hall after what happened the day before.

As they jogged down the high street,

Trey and Jax saw green vending machines everywhere. Practically one on every street corner.

Jax slowed down to catch his breath. "Hey, bro. Notice anything strange?"

Saturday afternoon was the busiest time for their local high street. The place should be buzzing with shoppers, traffic and that one dude with a megaphone who read the bible out in weekly instalments.

Trey nodded. "It's a ghost town."

Apart from a few pigeons pecking at the concrete, not a single living being disturbed the air. "Let's cut through the park," Trey said. The two boys changed direction so they could take their shortcut. But what they saw stopped them in their tracks.

The park was no more. The green, tree-lined recreation ground where they dawdled home after school was now a dusty grey desert.

The trees were bare apart from a few withered, colourless leaves.

Jax kicked at what used to be grass. It was dry as ash and crumbled beneath his feet. "It's just like what we saw on TV," he muttered.

Trey spun around. Where were the kids on the playground or the people walking their dogs? Where were the packed buses and cyclists and skateboarders? It was a Saturday afternoon in May, for goodness' sake. But now it was quieter than Christmas morning.

Trey put his hands to his mouth. "IS ANYONE OUT THERE?" he yelled.

Silence. The boys continued their journey.

Just as they passed their school, Jax saw someone up ahead. It was Dani. They both raced up to their friend. She was in her sports gear and looked confused to see them.

"Whoa, what's up with you guys?" she asked.

"Didn't you see our warning? Check the group chat!" Trey urged.

Dani held up her phone. "No can do. Signal's rubbish today, for some reason."

"You can't go home! It's not safe," Jax said.

The brothers explained what they saw that morning, including their parents' robotic transformation and the green vending machines that sprung up overnight.

Dani's face creased with concern. "I'd better call Mum and Ma, just to make sure everything's OK. They usually spend Saturdays at the allotment." Dani dialled home and put her phone to her ear. "I bet they never even saw…"

"What's up?" Trey asked.

"My stupid phone still isn't working! Can I use yours?" she said.

Trey and Jax got out their phones and tried to dial. But they didn't have any signal either.

"I'm not getting internet, wi-fi, anything," Trey said. "And my texts to Nate didn't send!"

Jax's eyes lit up. "This is the pattern! Oh man, why did I leave my notepad at home?" he muttered.

"What pattern, Jax? What's going on?" Dani asked.

He glared at them both. "I can't believe you guys. It's like you don't remember a thing I tell you! Am I just background noise to you?"

"We're listening now!" Dani said. "Tell us. Please."

Jax sighed. "I'm only telling you because it's mega important. While researching, I discovered a pattern. It didn't matter where they were in the world, everyone who reported the green flash and green hailstones just ... disappeared. No more updates."

"Because they lost their connection with the outside world," Dani said.

Jax shook his head. "They didn't lose anything. It was taken. On purpose."

"I don't know about that—" Trey began.

"Whatever's going on," Jax interrupted, "is much bigger than our neighbourhood."

The three friends looked at one another. Then, without saying a word, they turned on their heels and sprinted home.

18

They didn't stop running until their home loomed in the distance. The sight of their local park transformed into a grey dustbowl had them running even faster. It was the creepiest thing any of them had ever seen.

Trey, Jax and Dani arrived at the courtyard. Relief flooded through their veins as they saw familiar faces hanging around near the cat bench. They were even relieved to see Butterscotch.

Their friends were there. Judging by the

haunted expression on their faces, their grown-ups were acting strange too. Cameron chewed his nails anxiously while Madison, Layla and Chantelle paced the courtyard in their slippers. They'd clearly left home in a hurry.

Trey stopped to catch his breath. "Did … you guys … see … our … messages?" he said between gasps of air.

"Yes, but all of our phones stopped working before we could reply!" Layla said. "Trey, you won't believe what's happened."

"Let me guess? Your parents drank the free green coffee and are all acting strange?" Dani asked.

Madison nodded. "But it's not just our parents! My big sis—"

"And my aunties and uncles," Layla added. "They're all acting like—"

"Robots," Jax interrupted. "Just like the teachers and dinner ladies at school, right?"

Chantelle shook her head. "Nah. My mum's acting a bit odd, but she isn't on the rampage. Not like Crankshaw and the other teachers yesterday."

Jax cast his mind back to his research. If only he had his notepad!

"Let's all take deep, calming breaths," Dani said. "There's no need to start panicking."

Trey nodded. "Before we take our next move, we need to know the facts. One by one, tell us exactly what's going on with your grown-ups."

Madison and Chantelle's story were much the same as Trey and Jax's. Their grown-ups came home with coffee from the green vending machine that morning, and hadn't been acting right since.

But it was Cameron and Layla's stories that sent shivers down their spines. Their parents had been acting strange for a couple of days now, and had only been getting weirder and weirder.

"I told you that Dad started off saying the same sentence over and over," Layla said. "But then this morning, he got out of bed and just ... left. He didn't have his shoes on or anything."

"Mum did the same thing!" Cameron said. "I saw her leave from my bedroom window."

Where on earth had they gone? And could it explain why the high street was a ghost town? It was then that Jax realized something. "Guys. I have an idea, but I just need—"

"Not now, Jax. We're finally getting somewhere," Trey said dismissively. "So, we know that anyone who drinks the green coffee starts off a bit ... odd. But after a day or two, they go full haywire. Just like Crankshaw!"

"Yeah, you're right. I mean, the dinner ladies started off by serving up frozen bangers. But the next day they lobbed baked potatoes at anyone who stood in their way," Dani said.

"And after that, they disappear," Layla said. "Just like my dad."

Trey nodded. "They get hostile after a day or two. Which means we don't have much time left."

"This is what I've been trying to say," Jax said. "If I could just show you my notes, you'd see that—"

"Oh my gosh!" Chantelle shrieked. "I left Mum frying plantain at home. What if she burns the house down?"

"Your mum only drank the green coffee this morning, right?" Trey asked. "So, it's unlikely she's hostile yet. It's still safe for you to go home and check on her."

Dani nodded. "We should all do the same."

The squad agreed to go home and check on

their grown-ups. And, if possible to lock them in their bedrooms and keep them there until they could work out what was going on. The thought of sending their own parents to bed should have been funny. But it felt so strange.

They all formed groups: Trey went with Jax, Dani paired up with Madison, and Cameron joined forces with Chantelle and Layla.

"See you back here in half an hour, OK?" Trey said. "If anyone gets into trouble, just call. I mean, shout. Really loud."

"So, what do we do, bro?" Jax asked as they walked up the staircase to their flat. He could always count on Trey to have a plan.

"OK. We find Mum and Dad then put them in a safe part of the house. Somewhere they can't cause any accidents," he said.

Trey and Jax tentatively pushed the front door open. They could hear an odd bleeping sound coming from the kitchen. Was it coming from

Mum and Dad? They crept down the hallway and peeked through the open kitchen door.

Shopping bags were strewn over the floor and every cupboard door was left open. It was like they had abandoned everything halfway through unpacking the shopping.

Even the freezer door was open. Trey stepped inside the kitchen and closed it. The bleeping sound stopped, leaving the room eerily silent. Their parents were nowhere to be seen.

"Let's check the rest of the flat," Trey whispered to Jax.

The boys soundlessly crept into every room. They checked under beds, in wardrobes and even in the shower.

But the flat was empty. They knew it from the moment they stepped through the unlocked front door.

Trey raced through their options in his head, trying not to panic. Phones weren't working, so calling Nate, their grandparents or any other grown-up was out of the question.

"The neighbours! There's Mr and Mrs Patel, Lydia and that old guy with the cats," Trey said. "They'll know what to do."

"We should take … protection," Jax said.

After an unfruitful search (their flat was disappointingly low on armour), the brothers emerged with their weapons of choice. Trey clutched several wooden spoons sellotaped together to form a club, while Jax had both thumbs firmly fixed on two spray cans of whipped cream.

"If we have any trouble, I'll get 'em straight in the eyes. That should buy us some time," Jax said.

Trey nodded. Together, they walked to their closest neighbour and knocked firmly on the door.

The door swung open. It was unlocked.

That never happened. Even though the neighbours were friendly, it wasn't wise to leave your front door ... open.

Jax took a deep breath and marched into the flat, closely followed by Trey. They swept the flat, peering into every room. But there was that same deathly silence. They knew it was empty.

They checked every other front door on their level. They were all open.

Whatever happened to Mum and Dad had happened to their neighbours too. But before Trey and Jax could plan their next move, an ear-piercing scream froze the blood in their veins.

19

Trey and Jax raced outside, following the sharp sound of screams. Layla's face was a mask of horror as she pointed to something at the centre of the courtyard.

It didn't take long for the brothers to realize what was happening. The lush green bushes and flowers, so lovingly tended to by the older residents of Fernhill, were shrivelling before their eyes. In less than a minute, the green bush was withered and grey. The dried remains drifted away on the breeze.

"It's happening all over the neighbourhood!" Jax said. "You should see the park. It looks like a desert now."

"Forget the plants!" Trey said. "Where are the grown-ups? Every flat on our floor is empty."

"Don't you pay attention in biology, Trey? Without green plants, humanity is toast," Dani said.

Jax got his notepad out, the only thing he had taken from home, and scribbled down some notes. He was determined to pull together the pieces of this week.

Trey sighed. "Let's not jump to conclusions, OK? This day is weird enough without bringing in conspiracy theories."

The rest of their friends rushed outside to see what was going on.

"Did you find anyone at home?" Trey asked them.

They shook their heads. It seemed like they were the only ones in the entire estate.

"Mum left behind her handbag," Chantelle said. "It never leaves her side. Ever!"

Madison nodded. "My flat's empty too. But the car keys are in the usual spot."

"And can anyone get their phone working?" Trey asked.

"Of course not, Trey! They've shut down all lines of communication," Jax said. "I reckon it's an electro-magnetic signal that—"

"Stop right there," Trey said. "Who's *they*?"

Jax tried very hard not to roll his eyes. His big brother was usually smart. What wasn't clicking for him?

"We discussed this yesterday," Jax said. "The aliens!"

Trey sighed deeply. They were in the midst of a crisis, and Jax still couldn't shake his outlandish conspiracy theories.

"Aliens wouldn't be the wildest thing to happen this week, you know," Layla muttered.

Chantelle shuddered. "If only you lot saw the look in the dinner ladies' eyes yesterday. They were out for blood!"

"Look. I'm not saying that ... aliens aren't to blame. But it makes more sense to rule out more logical explanations first. Don't you think?" Trey said.

Dani nodded. "Agreed. We need to stay calm and avoid panicking."

"You sound just like a teacher," Jax said

"Thanks!" Dani took her role as the eldest and most sensible Fly High Crew squad member very seriously.

"It wasn't a compliment," Jax muttered.

"We should wait for my mums to come back from the allotment," Dani said. "They're usually here by now. You're all welcome to wait at my place, but I'll warn you: they might make you take home a bag of onions. We're drowning in them."

"They're not coming back from the allotment, Dani," Jax said. "No one is."

Cameron looked more worried than usual. "It's not like Mum to leave me without saying goodbye," he said quietly.

"Ignore Jax. Of course they're coming back. Cam, I bet your mum hasn't gone far at all," Trey said. It was his natural instinct to calm down his squad, whether they were nervous before a performance or just needed a reassuring word. But this time Trey's words seemed hollow.

A cloud covered the sun, leaving a faint chill in the air. It reminded the friends how late it was in the day. They hadn't seen a single grown-up all afternoon.

"Don't you get how much trouble we're in?" Jax asked. "We can't just hang around at Dani's waiting for someone to save us! No one listened to me when Crankshaw turned into the Terminator. No one listened to me about the green coffee. And you're **STILL** not listening to me now!"

"We're listening to you now, Jax," Madison said.

But Jax wasn't talking to the rest of the crew. He was talking to Trey.

"We believe you, Jax," Dani said quickly. "But it's not like there's proof or anything..."

"How much more proof do you need?" Jax scoffed. "We saw the green flash, the green hailstones, then the teachers went for us. Crankshaw's eyes glowed bright green, man. They looked like laser beams!"

"I don't know anything about Crankshaw's laser eyes," Trey said.

Jax looked hurt. "So, I'm a liar? Is that it?"

"Your mind is all over the place. You're not

a little kid, Jax!" Trey yelled. "When are you gonna grow up?"

Jax squared up to his brother. "Never! Not if it means becoming a boring know-it-all like you and Dani."

He ran upstairs back to their home, ignoring the shouts behind him. If Trey was so desperate for proof, then that's what he was going to get.

20

Trey's heart pounded like a pneumatic drill. He ran through his home, kicking in every door he passed. But all the rooms were empty and his family were nowhere to be found. He yelled their names and was taunted by his own echo.

Suddenly, there was a knock on the front door. A rhythmic pounding that didn't speed up or slow down. Trey stepped gingerly towards the door, which slammed open in his face. In the shadowy hall, two pricks of green light shone.

The figure stepped out of the shadows. "You're coming with me, boy," said a familiar voice. "I'll rid my school of you and your gang, if it's the last thing I do!"

Mr Crankshaw lunged towards Trey with his arms outstretched and green eyes ablaze.

"NO!" Trey screamed. He shot up in bed. As his eyes adjusted to the dark of his room, Trey realized the only thing touching him was the duvet.

The morning sunlight filtered through the curtains. He lay back in bed and took deep calming breaths, just like the instructor on Mum's yoga videos.

Mum. She was still gone, along with Dad and every other grown-up in Fernhill. Possibly their entire neighbourhood.

Yesterday was the weirdest day any of them had experienced. But Trey felt he had to hold it together for everyone else. After their fight, Jax wouldn't come out of his room for the rest of the night. When it became clear that none of the grown-ups were coming back home, Trey invited their friends back to his flat. He couldn't let them spend the night alone.

But unlike past sleepovers, there were no epic video game sessions, midnight feasts or practical jokes (not even that classic prank with the toilet and cling film). It was all they could do not to worry.

That probably explained Trey's vivid dream. He couldn't shake the image of Robo-Crankshaw lunging at him. Or the feeling that something was wrong.

Trey stepped over Cameron, who was snoring deeply from a sleeping bag on the floor, and made his way to Jax's room.

"Jax? You all right?" he asked.

No answer. Typical. Jax's stubborn trait

could really irritate Trey. Especially when he was making an effort to be reasonable.

"I'm coming in whether you like it or not," Trey said, pushing the door open.

The fresh morning breeze chilled the room and rustled the papers still sellotaped to the bedroom wall. Jax must have fallen asleep with the window open.

"Dad wouldn't like this," Trey muttered. Their dad thought that wasting heat was a cardinal sin. He hated when windows were left open overnight and the lights switched on in empty rooms. He reached over to shut the window.

"Yo, Jax, you awake?" Trey asked.

The Jax-shaped lump under the duvet was suspiciously still. He reached over to tap the bulge and it flattened under his hand. Trey pulled back the duvet.

Jax wasn't there. On his pillow lay a small

slip of paper. Trey unfolded it:

HAD TO FIND THE SOURCE.
BACK SOON. WITH PROOF.

The scrawled handwriting belonged to Jax. Trey had no doubt about it.

He wished more than anything he was wrong.

The rest of that Sunday flew by in a blur. Trey was determined to find Jax before his parents came back home.

Trey and his friends split into two search parties that scoured every floor in every building of their estate. Trey sat in the courtyard, the late afternoon sun burning bright on his face. If Mum was around, she'd be rubbing sunblock on his face.

He looked over at the green vending

machine, which was still there even if no one used it (there's nothing that would entice Trey or his friends to drink coffee). It stuck out like a sore, neon-green thumb.

Maybe Jax had a point? Coming up with an alien theory was typical of him. He just loved to take things too far. But Trey couldn't deny that this week had been weirder than anything he could have imagined.

"You can come out now, Jax!" Trey shouted. "You've made your point, OK?"

He saw Dani and a few other friends on the first-floor balcony and waved them down. From the look on her face, he could tell she didn't have good news.

"Any luck?" he asked.

She shook her head. "The girls and I must have knocked on every door. Unless Jax has found an invisibility cloak, he's not here, Trey."

"But we did find something else," Layla said.

Trey looked up. How did he miss that earlier?

Dozens of kids and teenagers peered down from the balconies on to the courtyard. He recognized their faces. They were his neighbours. People he'd seen around but never actually talked to.

"There isn't a single grown-up here," Chantelle said. "We're all alone."

"We spoke to a couple of them. They've been hiding at home ever since the grown-ups disappeared yesterday," Dani said. "They have no idea what's going on."

Trey nodded. He'd like to keep it that way. The last thing he needed was everyone panicking about aliens or conspiracy theories.

"Thanks for looking. I'm sure Jax'll turn up today. He's just annoyed with me 'cause I won't take his little alien theory seriously," Trey said.

"Speak for yourself," Chantelle scoffed. "My

mum won't even let me stay home by myself while she does the shopping. Aliens make more sense than her leaving me alone for the night with zero explanation."

Trey looked up at his friends. They weren't disagreeing.

"Look. We know Jax did a tonne of research, which is way unlike him," Dani said. "There's no harm in going through his notes and working out where he went next, is there?"

"I don't believe this," Trey muttered. "You're meant to be the sensible one."

The friends jogged upstairs and went back to Trey's flat. They spent the rest of the afternoon, and well into the evening, combing over Jax's room for clues. The internet was still down so they couldn't look at his laptop search history. In fact, like the TV and their phones, it wouldn't even switch on.

Instead, they relied on the hundreds of

handwritten notes, printed articles and various scribbles scattered around his room.

They discovered a lot about Jax: that he still slept with his raggedy comfort blanket under the pillow; that he favoured a blue biro pen; that there were socks under his bed so grimy that they probably counted as their own alien life form.

But they were still none the wiser about his location.

"I found it!" Chantelle yelled.

Trey stood up. "What, a clue about Jax?"

"No, my scented gel pen!" she said happily. "Jax borrowed it."

Trey sat back down, clearly disappointed.

"So Jax was really into the Amazon jungle, huh?" Layla asked. She sat cross-legged on the floor next to a stack of notes she was sorting through.

"That's where this 'alien' stuff all began,

according to him," Trey said. "He hasn't shut up about it all week."

"What did Jax's note say again?" Dani asked.

Trey took the crumpled paper out of his pocket. *"Had to find the source. Back soon."*

"The source of what?" Chantelle mused.

"I know where Jax is!" Dani shot up. "Follow me, everyone!"

21

Dani and Trey leaped on their borrowed bikes and pedalled to Park View High School. The rest of their friends wanted to come but Trey urged them to stay at home, just in case Jax turned up.

The sun had begun to set, casting a golden light over the school. They dismounted from their bikes and pushed them through the iron school gate. It creaked open.

Their schoolyard wasn't always the greenest place, but the shrivelled trees and bushes made the grey buildings look even more stark. Every tree was stripped of leaves and the hedges were little more than bundles of twigs. It was like locusts had come in their swarms and nibbled every bit of greenery in sight. "I can't even hear the birds," Dani whispered.

They silently pushed their bikes to the science block. Back to the source. It was where they saw the green flash on Tuesday night.

For Jax, it was the epicentre of the strange happenings from the last few days.

"Oh my gosh!" Dani said. She pointed to a white square on the ground.

When Trey got closer, he recognized it immediately.

"That's Jax's notepad, right?" she asked. "That means he can't be far!"

"Let's check Ms Appleby's shed. Maybe he tried to find her?"

They pushed their bikes past the science block towards the shed. That's when they noticed the buzzing sound.

Trey and Dani paused. The buzzing sound grew stronger.

"It's coming from down below," Dani whispered. She put down her bike and knelt on the concrete, ear hovering above the ground.

"Get up, Dani," Trey muttered. "You look so silly."

Dani ignored him. She followed the noise to its source: the back of the science block. Trey grumbled as he followed her. How come he always ended up on these wild goose chases?

The back of the science block was usually lined with deep green bushes. But all that was left was their skeletal grey remains. With the greenery gone, Trey and Dani noticed something for the first time: basement windows.

"I didn't realize the school had a basement," Dani said.

Trey reached over and pushed aside the grey twigs obscuring the windows. A green glow filtered through the glass. The buzzing sound was unmistakable now. It was coming from the basement.

"What do you see?" Dani asked.

"Just this weird green light. The twigs are in the way." Trey pulled at the brittle twigs and they snapped off in his hand. His eyes adjusted to the green glow coming from the window.

What he saw took his breath away. Trey leaped back like he'd seen a ghost.

Dani crouched down to look through the window. She gasped.

They saw Jax. But not like they'd ever seen him before.

Only his face was visible. The rest of Jax's body was cocooned in giant neon green leaves, wrapped tightly like a mummy. He was lying on the floor with his eyes closed.

"Is he ... he can't be..." Trey couldn't bring himself to say the words.

"It's OK," Dani said. "His chest is moving. He's still alive."

A dark flicker in the basement caught Trey's eye. "What the..." he muttered.

"Did you see that, too?" Dani whispered. He nodded.

They both crept towards the basement window and peered down. A dark silhouette moved slowly against the basement wall, sending a jolt of fear through Trey.

"Someone's in there!" he whispered.

Dani shook her head. "No way. That shadow is, like, fifteen feet tall. It can't be a person."

Trey gulped. "Maybe it's not a person."

The shadow paused long enough for Trey to make out a figure. It had very long arms, sharp pincers for hands, a narrow head and...

Trey gasped. "Are those ... antennae?"

It could only mean one thing. Jax had been right all along.

Dani's eyes widened with fear. "Trey. We should go. Whatever that thing is, it's not human."

"No way. I'm not leaving Jax alone with an alien!"

Trey got to his feet and stepped back. He

looked around for something, anything that could smash the window. He had to rescue his little brother from the creature that had him trapped.

Dani jumped up and sped over to her bike. "What are you waiting for? We need to move!"

"No way! I can't leave Jax here," Trey said.

"What are you gonna do? Kick your way

through a double-glazed window? And how are you taking on a giant alien alone? We need to go home and come back with reinforcements," Dani said.

Trey knew she was talking sense. But that didn't stop him feeling guilt and regret. If only he hadn't made Jax want to prove himself, he'd be at home right now.

If only Trey had listened.

"OK. Let's go back home, tell the squad and come back straight away," he said. Forming the backbone of a plan calmed him down.

The two friends sped off on their bikes through the darkened schoolyard.

22

Trey's alarm buzzed at 7.45 a.m. He showered, dressed and ate his cereal in a totally empty flat. No Jax moaning about getting up too early. No parents giggling over toast. No breakfast DJs on the radio in the kitchen. Was this his life now?

His heart thudded as he tied his school tie and laced up his black shoes. If Dad was here, he'd tell Trey that they needed polishing.

After what they saw last night, going to school seemed incredibly risky.

Straight after they saw the alien silhouette in the basement, Trey and Dani raced home to tell their friends. They came back with reinforcements (well, Dani's mum's toolkit), and planned to smash through the basement windows.

But when they got to the school, the gates were locked shut. There was no other way in.

Trey and his friends had to go back to school. Even if it meant crossing the paths of a giant alien. It was the only way to rescue Jax.

Just before he left the flat, Trey peered into Jax's room. The bedroom wall was still covered with Jax's research: maps, notes and news articles.

He sighed. "You were right, bro," Trey said to himself. "You were right."

Trey walked downstairs and met his friends in the courtyard outside their flats.

Dani held up her rucksack. "Don't worry,

Trey. I've got Mum's toolkit!"

"I can't believe you guys saw a real alien," Layla said, shaking her head.

"And in Fernhill of all places!" Chantelle said.

"Well, it was a shadow," Trey muttered.

"That shadow looked pretty convincing to me," Dani said.

"So Jax was right," Madison said. "The aliens, the green coffee, the teachers going haywire … it's all connected?"

Even though Trey saw Jax wrapped in the glowing green leaves and the creepy silhouette just last night, it still seemed far-fetched.

He walked up to the green vending machine in the courtyard. "I mean, it just looks like a normal vending machine to me. Has anyone actually looked at these things properly?"

Cameron shook his head. "No way. They give me the creeps!"

Trey walked around the vending machine, looking for something that would show it was just a normal coffee dispenser. Maybe a label from the manufacturer.

"Trey, don't you think it's weird that this vending machine is here with no electrical outlet?" Dani asked. "It's. Not. Normal."

"It could be underneath it," Trey said. He rolled up his shirtsleeves and pushed the vending machine. He pushed and shoved, throwing his entire body weight on to the machine. It didn't budge an inch.

Suddenly, the vending machine began to vibrate. Trey stepped back in shock. It rattled for several seconds before sinking slowly into the ground.

"Whoa!" Chantelle said. "Are you lot seeing this?" She ran towards the vending machine and her friends followed.

They watched as the green machine sank

smoothly into the ground, as though it was on an invisible elevator. When the vending machine disappeared completely, the red tile bricks of the courtyard meshed back together perfectly. After a few seconds, it was as though the vending machine never existed.

Dani gulped. "I think we know where that vending machine came from now. And it wasn't anywhere on earth."

The friends approached the school gates, and everything seemed normal from a distance. Students in their uniform milled about in the yard. But as they got closer, it was clear that the atmosphere was heavy.

The laughter, games and loud chatter was gone. Students huddled in small groups and talked in hushed tones. It was like someone had dialled the volume right down on every student in the school. Their mouths were moving but there was very little sound.

Trey and his friends shuffled through the schoolyard. Then he realized the students weren't talking. They were chewing.

Snacks were banned outside of lunch break in the schoolyard. But there wasn't a teacher in sight, so Trey guessed it made sense that students would have a sneaky bite to eat before lessons.

Out of the corner of his eye, Trey saw a flash of neon green. Then another. And another.

Every other student in the yard was clutching a handful of neon green balls. Then Trey realized.

"They're sweets!" he yelled.

Ignoring the confused questions of his friends, Trey raced to the edge of the yard where the coffee vending machine stood. It was gone.

In its place, stood neon green vending

machines. Five of them. But unlike last week, they didn't dispense green coffee. They dispensed sweets.

"No, no, no!" Trey watched with horror as cheerful students walked away with handfuls of marble-sized sweets wrapped in neon green paper. He didn't wait to see what would happen if his classmates ate them.

"Drop the sweets!" Trey yelled. "They're … they're … poisonous!" He ran in front of the nearest vending machine, blocking it. "The vending machines aren't safe!"

An older girl scowled at Trey. "Oi! You can't push in front of the queue."

"Yeah, back of the line!" another student yelled.

Dani appeared, trailed by the rest of their friends. The wide-eyed look of alarm on their faces told Trey that they understood what was happening. They were on his side.

"Trey's right!" Dani yelled. "The sweets are bad. They make you turn into … something else."

"IT'S THE ALIENS!" Cameron bellowed. His friends stepped back in shock. None of them had ever heard him raise his voice, let alone shout at the top of his lungs.

The schoolyard paused for a second. Then

they cracked up laughing.

"Yo! These lot belive in aliens!" someone cried.

Trey's cheeks burned with humiliation. *This is how Jax must have felt*, he thought.

The friends watched helplessly as their classmates chomped on the chewy green sweets.

"Maybe we made a mistake?" Dani asked. "Nothing's happening."

Then the bell rang. Every single student dropped their heads. When they looked up, their eyes flashed green.

They spoke in unison, tinny voices echoing in the schoolyard. "Activating. Pupil. Mode."

The robo-students moved like an army and filed through the school entrance one by one. Trey, Dani and their friends huddled behind a vending machine and watched their classmates shuffle into the grey building.

"Look, it's the entire school," Layla whispered. "They're all … one of them!"

"I say we go home," Madison said. "It's got to be safer than spending a day with actual robots. What if they go haywire like on Friday?"

Trey shook his head. "I'm not leaving without Jax. You lot can do what you like."

"Good morning, students." The friends turned to find a familiar figure towering behind them. It was Ms Tackle.

Trey clocked that her voice was smoother and less tinny than the robo-teachers they saw last week. Her movements weren't as stiff, too. It was as though the robots were upgraded over the weekend to make them seem more natural.

It meant that someone, or something, was behind all of this.

"Continue to period one. Immediately," Robo-Tackle said.

The friends were too terrified to speak. Whatever just happened to the students of Park View High School? The teachers were surely in on it. If they talked and moved like themselves, who knew what Robo-Tackle would do to them.

Dani bolted upright. Then she turned at an angle and walked in shuddering steps towards the queue of students, joining at the end. Trey and their friends followed her lead. Keeping up this act was the only way to survive.

It was going to be a long day.

23

That morning was turning out to be the Monday of nightmares. Worse than a rainy walk to school, forgetting your PE kit and double maths combined.

Trey knew he had to mimic his classmates. It wasn't in his nature to copy others, but it was the only way to avoid being caught out. He had to blend in.

He shuffled into French and took his usual seat while Mr Camembert did the register. The students flipped open their textbooks in unison, all landing on the exact same page. Trey copied. While they read in silence about Pierre's trip to the train station, the door swung open.

"Sorry I'm late, Sir," Kwame said. He was one of Trey's classmates. And by the sound of his voice, definitely not a robot.

Trey's heart jumped to his throat. He had no idea how Mr Camembert would act.

The teacher stood up slowly and pointed to the door. "Out. Student."

Kwame rolled his eyes. "But, Sir! I'm only five minutes late."

He was only getting sent out? That was a relief. Trey kept his eyes on the textbook like everyone else while Kwame stood outside. Mr Camembert followed with a handful of green sweets in his hand.

Trey realized what was about to happen. But if he got up to warn Kwame, they were both stuffed. He stayed seated, his heart racing as he listened to the conversation outside the door.

"No thanks, Sir. I had breakfast already," he heard Kwame say. Mr Camembert replied in quiet tones and Trey couldn't hear exactly what was being said but it sounded like an argument.

There was a short, muffled scream. No one else in the class reacted.

Then, quiet. That silence was more chilling than anything else Trey had heard.

The whole thing was over in one minute. Mr Camembert returned to his desk while Kwame trailed behind him. He joined a table near Trey, got out his textbook and silently flipped it to the right page.

If Trey dared to look up, he would have seen Kwame's eyes flash green.

It wasn't until lunchtime that Trey was reunited

with Dani and his friends. They met near the science block. Once they were obscured by the squat grey building, they dropped their robot act. Robo-teachers patrolled the school yard while students sat quietly on benches.

"It was so scary," Cameron said. "Mrs Upton came to check on our classroom and handed the teacher more green sweets. I pretended to drop my pencil and ducked under the table."

Suddenly, a head peeked around the corner. It was Logan.

The Fly High Crew had been caught out by none other than the school bully.

"Back off, Logan!" Dani yelled, and lobbed her (very heavy) rucksack at his head. "OWWWWW!" Logan yelled and staggered back. That wasn't the

reaction they expected.

"Wait. You're not a robot?" Dani said.

"No!" Logan said, clutching his nose.

"What do you want now, Logan?" Trey said. "Because I'm really not in the mood for your petty insults!"

"Chill out, yeah? I came to find you guys. I think we're the only ones that haven't turned completely bonkers."

Trey relaxed a little. "So you didn't eat the sweets?"

Logan shook his head. "Nope. I'm diabetic. Mum would lose her rag if I had sugar before ten a.m. Why didn't you lot eat the sweets?"

"Because of the aliens!" Cameron blurted out.

Logan's face crumpled with laughter. "You can't be serious!"

"Deadly," Trey said.

"Did your grown-ups disappear on Saturday

too? And don't tell me you didn't notice that every scrap of grass has dried up. In two days!" Dani said.

Logan stopped laughing. "It's been a weird weekend. But... aliens?"

"You can see for yourself, if you want," Trey said. "Follow me."

Logan followed Trey and his friends to the back of the science block.

"Now, what you're going to see might be upsetting," Trey said gravely. "But you've got to remember that Jax is just in a deep sleep."

"Do you need the tools, Trey?" Dani asked. She fished around in her rucksack. "I took Mum's electric drill."

Logan rubbed his sore nose. "Cor. I'm lucky you didn't break it," he muttered.

"In a sec," Trey said. "Have a look through the basement window and see for yourself."

Everyone stepped closer. "I can't see anything,

Trey," Chantelle said.

"I just see the floor," Madison agreed.

Trey rolled his eyes. "Then you're not looking hard enough! I'll show you." He dropped to his knees and peered through the basement window.

The room was empty. No bundle of giant leaves, no green glow and definitely no Jax.

"B–but Jax was here last night! We saw him!" Trey panicked. He kicked the window but the glass didn't budge.

If Jax wasn't in the basement, then where on earth could he be?

Logan folded his arms. "So where's this proof, eh?"

"Pupil! Cease damaging school property. Immediately."

The group spun around with their backs to the wall. In front of them stood Crankshaw with several blank-faced students. Unlike the students, his eye glowed a menacing green.

"Take them away," Crankshaw said.

The students whipped off their school ties and stepped towards Trey and his friends. They were cornered; there was no escape.

The last thing Trey saw before being blindfolded was Crankshaw's piercing green stare.

24

A strong grip held Trey's shoulders firmly in place as he was forced across the schoolyard. At least, he assumed it was the schoolyard. Thanks to the blindfold he wasn't totally sure.

"HELPPPPPPP!" Dani screamed.

Heck, it was worth a try. Trey screamed for help as well. He and his captured friends filled the schoolyard with their screams.

It was a waste of time. No one came to help or even reacted. They were truly alone.

After a few minutes, they paused. Trey heard

a jangly sound and the scrape of metal against metal. He was pushed into a cool, dark room that smelled of fumes like petrol. Was there a garage on the school grounds they didn't know about?

The door slammed. Trey heard the voice of Mrs Upton through the door. "Insubordinate pupils must be dealt with," she said in that strange tinny voice. As though she was talking through a fuzzy speaker.

"Yes, head teacher," Crankshaw said. Then Trey heard the clack of their shoes against the concrete fade into the distance.

It felt like hours passed before anyone in the shed spoke.

Trey lifted off his blindfold. "I think the coast is clear," he whispered.

"Is everyone OK?" Dani asked.

Chantelle, Layla, Cameron, Madison and Logan said they were fine. But like Trey, they were shaken up by the experience.

"Where are we? And why does it smell like a farm in here?" Layla said.

Apart from tiny rays of light shining through chinks in the wall, the room was completely dark. There were no windows either.

"Who knows?" Dani said. "Apparently this school has back doors and secret tunnels." She thought back to their escape from the PE hall on Friday. There was lots she didn't know about the school.

A gurgling sound pierced the quiet.

Trey jumped to his feet. "What was that?!"

"It was me," Cameron said sheepishly. "I skipped lunch."

Dani carefully stood up and walked over to the locked door. "Guys, we haven't got much time. I bet Crankshaw will be back as soon as the home time bell rings. And I don't wanna be here when he arrives."

She tugged and tugged at the handle. The padlock outside rattled but the door didn't budge. They were well and truly locked in.

"It doesn't make any sense," Layla said. "What do aliens want with Fernhill? There's nothing exciting here. Like, at all."

Layla was right. Apart from being home to the country's loudest cat (the owner had a certificate to prove it), nothing of note ever happened in Fernhill. The most exciting thing about the place was leaving it.

"And it's not like we have natural resources. Because that's what aliens usually want, right? No oil, gold, diamonds…" Dani said.

"Hey, Trey," Chantelle said. "Did Jax have any idea why the aliens are here?"

Trey felt a pang of guilt at hearing Jax's name. So far, his idea to heroically bust his little brother out of the school basement was not going to plan.

"He was obsessed with the Amazon rainforest," he replied. "Jax said that the green hailstones appeared there first, as well as other places. Like Australia, Costa Rica … can't remember the last one."

If only I'd paid more attention, Trey thought.

"Then what?" Layla asked.

"Then nothing," Trey said. "All updates from those areas stopped. Total blackout."

"Just like here," Cameron muttered. "My phone hasn't worked since Saturday."

"Let's assume that the same thing that happened here is happening elsewhere. Straight after the blackout, grass starts to disappear, right?" Dani said.

"Not just grass!" Madison said. "Trees, bushes, hedges…"

"And spabbages!" Dani yelled. "But of course."

"Spabbages? I think this one needs some

fresh air," Layla muttered. "She's making up words, now."

"Guys, I have an idea. I need you all to stay very still," Dani said. "I'll try not to step on your toes."

The crew heard clatters and bangs as Dani felt her way to the back of the room, knocking down untidy shelves in the process.

"I knew it!" she yelled from the back of the room. "We're not in the school at all. We're in Ms Appleby's shed."

"Yes!" Trey yelled, feeling hopeful for the first time that day. "If we're in the shed, that means…"

"…There's a trapdoor," Dani said. "I can feel it here. But without Ms Appleby's keys, we're not getting out."

Trey dimly remembered the creaky wooden door hidden beneath a sheet of tarpaulin. "Nah, we've got this, Dani!"

He crawled to the back of the shed and rolled up his sleeves. "I'll take it from here."

If the shed wasn't pitch black, Trey would have seen Dani roll her eyes.

Trey pulled at the trapdoor handle, grunting with the exertion. The rickety trapdoor was more secure than it looked.

"Mind if I have a try?" Logan said. "Us rugby lads have more upper body strength, after all."

"Fine," Trey said through gritted teeth. "I've loosened it up for you, anyway."

Logan wrenched the door upwards with all of his might. But he had no luck either.

"It's done for," he said. "There's no way we're getting out of this—"

A whirring sound interrupted him. It was Dani's electric drill, which had been in her rucksack all along.

"Step aside, boys," Dani said. Groping in

the dark, she found the screws fastening the lock to the trapdoor. It was fiddly work, but she was able to unfasten them one by one.

Then, the bell rang.

"That means home time," Madison said. "Crankshaw could be here any minute!"

"I'm going as fast as I can!" Dani said.

"Let's block the door with this old junk," Chantelle said. "Quickly!"

The squad grabbed anything they could find – rusting toolboxes, tins of paint, rickety shelves – and put them against the door. It would hold off Crankshaw for a few minutes. If they were lucky – this upgraded Robo-Crankshaw seemed far more sophisticated than the one they faced a few days ago.

Finally, the last screw whirred out of its fastening. Dani yanked off the padlock and flipped the trapdoor open.

"Follow the tunnel to the other side!" she

said, urging the rest of Fly High Crew down first. They crawled into the dirt-covered hole one by one.

A jangling sound rang from the other end of the shed. Crankshaw's keys.

"Move, move, move!" Trey whispered.

He heard the padlock on the shed door release. A chunk of daylight seeped through the door as it began to creep open. The pile of junk on the other side of the door blocked it.

"Pupils must not obstruct the doors. Desist immediately." Crankshaw's tinny voice rang through the shed.

Just as Dani's ankles wriggled through the tunnel and out of sight, Trey dived in after her. He flipped the trapdoor back down after him before following his friends through the earthy hole, the sound of junk crashing to the floor loud in his ears.

25

Trey hauled himself out of the tunnel and on to the small patch of land. The allotment was unrecognizable. What was left of the spabbages had turned into dust, and the lush green hedges were now a bundle of twigs. Ms Appleby would have been heartbroken.

"We've got to move quick," Dani whispered. "It's only a matter of time before Crankshaw finds the tunnel and comes after us!"

"But where to?" Madison asked. "We're trapped!"

A red brick wall separated them from the outside world. Beyond that, the old factory towered above them. Trey had never noticed it before because of the greenery.

He pointed to the abandoned building. "Do you reckon we could hide out there?" Trey said. "The teachers would never think to check."

"Er, is there another tunnel out of here that I don't know about?" Layla said. "Because I

don't see how we're gonna scale a ten-foot brick wall."

Dani had already whipped off her blazer. She ran back, then launched herself up the wall with her chest raised high. Her hands gripped the top of the wall and she hauled herself up. It happened in seconds.

The rest of the squad couldn't help but be impressed. "One down, six to go!" Dani said, beaming from the top of the wall.

Cameron shook his head. "There's no way I can do that."

"That's no way to think!" Madison chirped. "If you really try, you'd be surprised at what you can achieve."

"Madison's right," Dani said. "You might not be able to free-run like me. But there must be something you can do. C'mon, think!"

Then the answer hit Trey. "Let's form a human pyramid! We tried it in rehearsal, once."

Half of the crew knelt on all fours while the other half launched off their backs. The height boost meant they could grab the top of the brick wall and haul themselves up, just like Dani.

Then, working as a team, the top crew reached down and hauled the others up in pairs.

"See, you did it!" Dani said.

But there was no time for congratulations. "Er, how do we get down?" Logan asked.

Trey peered at the hard concrete below. He didn't need a physics degree like Nate to know that jumping wasn't an option. Not if they wanted to keep their ankles intact.

"Look at the green vans over there! We can shimmy down then climb on to them," Dani said.

The crew shuffled down the wall until they reached the cluster of green vans parked against the brick wall. One by one, they carefully jumped on to the van roof, then slid down from a safer height.

Apart from Dani, who leaped down the wall and tumbled into a ball on the ground with ease.

"Show-off," Trey smirked as she dusted herself off.

Dani smiled. "What? You mean Fernhill's next free-running champion can't have a little fun?"

"That was amazing!" Logan said breathlessly. "I thought scaling that wall was impossible. But we did it!"

"Bit different from rugby, eh?" Trey said.

"Y'know, I always wanted to join Fly High Crew," Logan said sheepishly. "But my big bro teased me about it. He said that boys shouldn't dance."

"No offence, Logan, but your big bro sounds

like an idiot," Trey said.

"I thought this place was abandoned," said Cameron, pointing at the smoke puffing from the chimneys.

They looked up at the red-brick building that towered above them. The top windows were smashed and graffiti adorned the walls. It certainly looked abandoned, but the car park packed with green vans and the chimney smoke proved otherwise.

"We just need somewhere to hide and catch our breath. Throw the robo-teachers off our scent," Trey said.

"Wait! We can't go in without protection." Dani tumbled the contents of her mum's toolkit on to the ground. But besides the electric drill, there wasn't much in there of use.

Trey held up a ball of rubber bands. "Seriously, Dani?"

"What am I meant to do with this?"

Cameron asked, holding up a tape measure.

"Use your imagination!" she said.

Together, the crew slipped through a side door and made their way into the whirring hive of the factory.

26

The sound inside the factory was close to deafening. This place was anything but abandoned.

The crew looked up in wonder at the gleaming stainless-steel construction before them. Barrels and pipes towered several storeys upwards, illuminated by giant windows letting in the late afternoon sunlight. A conveyor belt wrapped the length of the factory floor.

"Does anyone know what sort of factory this is?" Cameron asked, raising his voice to be heard over the machinery.

Dani shook her head. "This place has been empty for as long as I can remember. At least, I thought it was empty."

"Check out this equipment," Trey said. "It's so shiny. Like it's hardly been used."

Suddenly, there was a whooshing sound. It came from a giant pipe in the centre of the factory. The friends backed up against the wall, ready to make a quick getaway.

A stream of neon green balls shot out from the pipe, filling large cardboard boxes on a conveyor belt.

The belt inched forward when each cardboard box was full, replacing it with an empty one. It seemed like the supply of sweets tumbling down the pipe would never end. Another machine slapped a white label on each cardboard box and pushed it on to a crate on the floor.

"Wait a sec!" Chantelle said. "Are those…"

"The sweets!" Trey yelled. "We've stumbled straight into their factory!'

"This place isn't safe. We need to go," Dani said.

"Not yet. Whoever's planning this is trying to expand," Layla said. "We have to find out where!" Before anyone could stop her, she squeezed through the tight space under the conveyor belt and crawled to the opposite end of the factory.

"What is that girl playing at?!" Dani said.

Layla stood over the piles of cardboard boxes. "They're going all over the place!" Layla yelled over the whirr of the factory machines. "France. Japan. Canada. It's total domination!"

Trey gulped. It was one thing knowing his neighbourhood had been taken over by aliens.

But the entire world? They had to stop the sweets going out, otherwise they'd be the only normal ones left.

Suddenly, the sound of buzzing competed with the whirring of the factory floor. The far wall of the factory began to raise. That's when they realized that it wasn't a wall at all. They were shutters.

"Hide, Layla!" Trey yelled. The rest of the crew ducked beneath the conveyor belt.

Layla slipped behind a stack of cardboard boxes. The shutters revealed the backs of several green vans, just like the ones parked outside, with wide open doors.

Pistons beneath the crates pumped up and slid the sealed boxes into the vans. They watched with horror as Layla's crate was also pushed into the van. With her in it.

"She's stuck!" Dani said. "What do we do?"

"It's gonna be OK," Trey said. "I think we've got some time before they leave."

The van doors slammed shut at exactly the same time. Their engines rumbled.

"Or not," Cameron said.

Stopping the van meant revealing themselves to the aliens. Trey had no choice. Before he could change his mind, he ran into the car park.

He made it outside just as the convoy of green vans prepared to leave the factory grounds. Up ahead, the heavy iron gate shuddered open. There wasn't much time.

"Helpppp!" Layla's muffled voice came from the van at the front.

He jogged behind it and banged on the door. No response. The driver kept it moving. How else was he going to get their attention?

Trey reached for the rubber band ball in his pocket, swung his arm back and took aim. The wing mirror smashed and the vans screeched to a halt.

The driver's doors on all the vans opened in unison. Figures dressed in bright green overalls stepped out of their vehicles. The men moved as one with a coordination that looked superhuman. They were totally in sync.

Five pairs of eyes were focused on Trey. Two of the men in green overalls staggered towards him wordlessly, gripped him by his shoulders and marched him towards the front gate.

Trey was secretly relieved. There were worse fates than being kicked out of the factory. He could go home, find the other kids at Fernhill and rescue his friends with back-up.

Suddenly, a crackling sound dominated the factory car park. The two men pushing Trey stopped to listen. He realized it came from a tannoy.

The tinny voice boomed across the car park. "Trespassers to report to Room 101. Immediately."

The two men rotated Trey and pushed him towards another corner of the car park. Dread pooled in his stomach as Trey realized he was nowhere near his friends.

Out of the corner of his eye, Trey saw another two men in green overalls marching Layla in the opposite direction. She had escaped the crate, but at what cost?

The two men marched Trey to a darkened corner of the car park. He heard the rumbling of the factory wall through the red brick wall. Why were they taking him to some corner?

Then, the heavy metal doors of a cellar hatch swung open, as if pushed by invisible hands. Now he knew exactly what they were going to do.

He wrestled and jostled, trying to free himself from the iron grip of his guards. He screamed, shouted and dug his heels into the ground. But his captors didn't even flinch.

They reached the edge of the hatch. Inky darkness yawned below. He was done for.

Moving in unison, the two guards lifted Trey

up by his waist as though he were weightless. They hovered him over the hole while his legs dangled in the air.

Then, they let go. And Trey was too shocked to even scream.

27

Trey landed on the ground with a thump.
Something firm and bouncy broke his fall.
Must have been an old sofa. Whatever it was,
he was grateful for it. That could have been
his dancing career over before it had begun.

"I'm OK. I'm alive," he said. Saying it out
loud confirmed that he wasn't a bundle of
broken bones. Although his bum was kind
of sore.

Clank. The guards slammed the cellar hatch
shut, leaving Trey in the dark. He carefully

stood up and stretched. Terrifying as it was to be thrown down here, Trey was relieved that the steely grip of the guards no longer rested on his shoulders.

Why had he come after Layla instead of sticking with the rest of the crew?

Because she would have done the same for you. They all would.

As his eyes adjusted to the darkness, Trey noticed that he hadn't fallen on an old sofa. He ran his hands along the cool, slightly prickly surface.

It was a plant. Maybe several of them. The sort with lush leaves thicker than his forearm. They weren't like any of his mum's houseplants, or anything he'd seen before, in fact.

Maybe they were the same leaves Jax was wrapped in? Trey jumped off the leaves before he was wrapped into a cocoon, just like Jax. But discovering the leaves gave him hope for the first time all day. Jax could be close.

Trey just had to find a way out.

He shuffled around the cellar, feeling his way through the darkness. Trey was drawn to a trail of fine green dust on the floor. It glowed brighter and brighter, casting its light across the ground. It seemed to point the way.

He picked up a handful of the green particles. On closer inspection, it wasn't dust at all. It looked just like the green hailstones he found at the school with Dani and Jax. They were cool to the touch, although far from icy, and they didn't melt in his hand.

Jax was right. Whatever they were, it wasn't normal for them to be raining from the sky.

Trey followed the trail of glowing green hailstones across the cellar and through a narrow tunnel that looked like an air ventilation shaft. There was light at the other end of this tunnel, and Trey scampered towards it gratefully.

Trey stuck his head out of the tunnel and took in the view. It totally defied his expectations.

The cylindrical room was several storeys high. Battered metal sheets covered the walls and the roof was a series of glass windows misted with condensation. The roof was so high up that the late afternoon sunlight struggled to penetrate the rest of the room. The room was eerily silent apart from the faint whirr of machinery. He couldn't be too far from the factory floor, yet this chamber felt completely different from the rest of the building.

For one, it was warmer and damper than any weather Trey had ever experienced.

Still on all-fours, Trey looked down. He was shocked to see that the tunnel opened on to a steep drop. Not even Dani could have scaled that. The base of the room was covered with exotic-looking green plants, so dense that Trey couldn't see the floor.

There was no logical reason why the old sweet factory would have a greenhouse. This was definitely the work of extra-terrestrials, Trey realized with a shudder.

There was a ladder attached to the tunnel leading into the green depths below. Trey shook it and it didn't rattle. It seemed secure enough. He took a deep breath and carefully stepped down the iron steps until he reached the jungly depths.

The base of the room was damp-smelling, dark and very warm. It reminded Trey of his school trip to the botanical gardens, where the greenhouses felt like a jungle. He rolled up his shirtsleeves.

The structure in the centre of the room was impossible to miss. Several glowing green leaves stood upwards, each leaf taller than Trey, and pointed towards the ceiling, in a semi-circle. They looked like the same sort of leaves that Trey landed on: thick, rubbery and not of this world. The way they were arranged reminded him of a fence. Or a prison gate. This plant pen rested on more glowing green leaves, unfurling like a giant flower.

The size of the plant alone (it was easily taller than the brick wall they had just scaled) made Trey realize it was not of this world. If it wasn't so unsettling to see an alien plant, it would have been beautiful.

Trey wiped his brow and breathed deeply. It felt like there wasn't enough air in the room. Suddenly, the plant prison twitched.

Something was inside.

"You've got this, Trey," he muttered to himself. Resisting the urge to hot-foot it back up the ladder, Trey circled the green plant prison until he reached the other side of the room. He had to know what he was dealing with.

The tall green plants rustled and swayed. Trey knew for sure he wasn't alone.

"What are you and where's my little brother?!" he shouted.

Silence. Then, a snapping sound. The tall plants moved aside to reveal a glowing centre.

"Hello, Trey," a voice came from up above.

Trey blinked as the glowing centre lit up the room. "No way," he muttered.

"Way," said the voice.

It belonged to Jax. With the tall plants parted, Trey saw his brother perched majestically on a glowing green-leaf throne. He looked nothing like the small, weak boy he'd seen cocooned in the school basement.

This Jax was dressed all in green leaves fashioned to form a vest and shorts. Then Trey realized that it wasn't a vest. It was armour.

And did Jax have biceps now?

It was obvious. The aliens had kidnapped his little bro for their grim experiments.

"They got you, too?" Trey groaned. "I thought you were too clever to eat the sweets, Jax! But don't worry, I'm gonna rescue you—"

Jax's booming laugh cut Trey off. Despite the sub-tropical heat, his blood chilled in his veins. He'd never heard his little bro laugh like that.

"Why would I eat one of the green sweets? In case you forgot, *I* was the one that warned *you*," Jax said. "Not that you listened."

He had a point. Trey noticed that Jax didn't have the tinny voice or glass-eyed stare that the other students had after eating the green sweets.

"What did they do to you?" Trey said. "We saw you in the school basement and tried to rescue you!"

"Did you know those little green sweets were my idea?" Jax said, ignoring Trey's question. "The newcomers had to make sure the children didn't interfere with their plans. And free coffee wasn't going to work, was it?"

Trey's face screwed up with disgust. Jax had betrayed their whole town. And for what?

"Why would you help them? They've turned all the grown-ups into robots, you know. Crankshaw's worse than ever!"

Jax looked remorseless. He examined his fingernails. "Yes. Well, the newcomers promised to get Crankshaw out of the way. If I helped them, they said no one would ever pick on me again."

"The Jax I know wouldn't sell out his squad," Trey spat.

Jax slowly rose to his feet. The crown of his head towered over the tall leaves. There was no doubt about it: he had grown several inches in two days.

"The Jax you know doesn't exist any more," he boomed.

Trey's eyes widened in shock.

"You know what I love about these newcomers, Trey? They recognize what's in here," Jax said, tapping his temple. "They actually listen to me," Jax continued. "Unlike my family or my so-called squad. You ignored me. Teased me. Made me feel tiny."

"W-we've been so worried about you, bro," Trey stammered.

"Save it!" Jax yelled. "I don't need your concern. I'm basically their leader now."

Trey shook his head in disbelief. "Jax … you can't be serious!"

He frowned. "Why's that such a shock, huh? Because I'm the leader for a change? Because they didn't pick you? Typical."

"Bro, that's not what I meant," Trey replied.

His voice dropped to a whisper. "These aliens are evil, man. They're planning something big!"

"Did you know that I'm the only person on the entire planet that got close to discovering their plan?" Jax said.

Trey was still reeling from his shocking discovery. But he had to know.

"What's their plan? Is anything ever going back to normal?" he asked.

Jax was silent. A sly smile crept on to his face.

"The newcomers would like to show you themselves."

28

Trey was about to see aliens. Actual beings from outer space! He braced himself for a horrifying sight. The enormous shadow he saw in the basement was scary enough. How much more terrifying would they be face to face?

A buzzing sound filled the humid room. It took a second for Trey to realize it was coming from the giant plant. The air around him vibrated as small green specks rose from the alien leaves.

"It's the hailstones," Trey realized.

The tiny green pearls ascended into the air, filling every corner of the room up to the glass ceiling. There must have been thousands. No, millions.

Then they changed course, flying like neon green insects, and rested on the curved metal wall.

Trey had never seen hail move like that before. It buzzed and swarmed with a life of its own.

"W-what are they?" Trey stuttered.

Jax smirked. "They're the aliens, of course."

Trey looked bewildered. "But they're tiny! I could fit dozens of them in the palm of my hand!"

This was their enemy? Trey and his friends could destroy them with water from a hosepipe.

"Alvin, this is Trey. Trey, meet Alvin," Jax said. "Are you gonna say hello or what, Trey?"

He waved slowly to the wall of buzzing

green aliens. Suddenly, the buzzing green wall moved. They shuffled like a school of fish, rearranging themselves until they formed a moving shape. It was a human hand, and it waved back.

"Pretty sweet, huh?" Jax said.

Trey was speechless. He nodded.

Jax sat down on his throne of glowing leaves. "The newcomers are from a planet that is untranslatable to any Earth languages. So, I named them Alvin and they're cool with it."

Alvin shifted from the waving hand to form a giant thumbs-up. It seemed like Alvin really was cool with it.

"They're from a galaxy far, far away. If you take a left from the Milky Way and drive for nine hundred trillion light years, you can't miss it," Jax continued. "Alvin said their planet used to be a beautiful place."

The swarming green mass shuffled on the

wall. In a few seconds, the image became an alien terrain lush with greenery. The plants swayed on the breeze and the moving image teemed with life. Trey was blown away by the detail. It was like watching a movie clip.

"But then they ran out of food," Jax said.

Alvin changed again. Gone was the lush greenery and plant life. Now that same terrain was dry, dusty and bare.

"Just like our neighbourhood," Trey said.

"Quiet. We're not finished," Jax said sternly. "As I was saying. The newcomers turned to their neighbours across the galaxy for help."

Alvin reformed to show a fleet of rockets hurtling past stars and planets. It felt so realistic that it made Trey dizzy.

"Finally, after a long journey, they came across Earth. Lush, fertile Earth. We have more than our fair share of green fuel," Jax said. "Alvin landed on the greenest places, and—"

"Fuel? I thought you said they wanted food?" Trey asked.

Jax glared. "I don't like it when you interrupt. Neither does Alvin."

"Sorry," Trey muttered. "But something isn't adding up. I understand why the aliens landed in the Amazon. But why Fernhill? No jungles round here."

Jax was quiet and nodded his head. He was clearly having a silent conversation with Alvin, which Trey found incredibly creepy. How were they communicating?

He chuckled. "But, of course. We have Ms Appleby to thank for that."

Alvin formed the image of a giant green plant. A whole row of them. Trey recognized them immediately: they were spabbages!

"Alvin says that the plant we call 'spabbages' are a unique life form unlike any other in the galaxy," Jax said. "They just had to try them."

So, because of a mutant spinach-cabbage hybrid, their entire neighbourhood was under threat by aliens the size of aphids? Trey's head was spinning.

"But our new friends only want enough plant life to sustain them. We won't even miss it."

"Rubbish!" Trey yelled. "There isn't a single green plant left out there. You saw what they did to our neighbourhood. They've taken every scrap of green there is."

The buzzing in the room lowered in tone. It sounded menacing.

"Alvin says that's a lie," Jax said. "Besides, Earthlings clearly don't look after the green they have. The atmosphere is horribly polluted and they tear down millions of precious trees every day. If you won't value it, then we will."

"If your new friends are so harmless, why have they turned everyone but us into senseless robots, eh? Ask Alvin what they've done to Mum and Dad!" Trey yelled. "And while you're at it, ask Alvin why mind-control sweets are being shipped to every city in the country!"

Jax shot up from his throne. "Alvin says it's temporary!"

"You believe that?" Trey said.

"Why shouldn't I believe them? In just a couple of days, Alvin's given me everything I ever wanted," he said, flexing his muscles. "If I help them with their plan, I'll never deal with another bully again."

"You don't have to go through with this, bro," Trey said quietly.

Jax frowned. "That's so easy for golden boy Trey to say," he spat. "You're not the one who's ignored. You're not the one who's teased."

"So what? We all get teased from time to time. That's life!" Trey said.

Jax's face turned to thunder. "You. Have.

No. Idea. None! Why would I go back to a life where I'm constantly second-best?"

"I don't believe this!" Trey yelled. "Do you know what I risked to rescue you?"

Jax crossed his arms and peered down at his brother from his glowing throne. "Typical Trey. Always thinking that he's gotta come to the rescue, eh? I didn't ask for your help."

"I'm not leaving without you," Trey said.

"Then prepare to be disappointed. Because I'm never going back. Not to school. Not to home. And not to Fly High Crew."

"Jax! Stop being so stubborn," Trey yelled. He couldn't imagine going home without him.

The buzzing sound in the room intensified. "What's that, Alvin?" Jax said. He was silent for a few seconds. "I see."

"What's going on?" Trey asked.

"Tell your squad that there's no point in hiding on the factory floor." Jax said. "You're dismissed."

A creaking sound came from the wall and grabbed Trey's attention. A set of shutters rose, revealing a small cubby hole just big enough for one person.

"Your ride is here," Jax smirked. The green leaves surrounding his throne slid into place, hiding him from view.

"Jax, I can't leave without you!" Trey yelled.

Suddenly, the tiny aliens flew away from the wall. Trey watched as they formed an angry swarm. Then they flew at him.

It was like being in the midst of a green tornado. The tiny aliens whirled around Trey, spinning and spinning until he felt sick with dizziness.

"Whoaaaargh!" Trey screamed. His feet left the ground and the alien horde tossed him into the metal lift like he was a piece of garbage.

Then, the shutters came down on him.

29

It was a good thing Trey wasn't claustrophobic. The shutters went down on the tiny cubbyhole leaving him in near-darkness, apart from the glow of the UP and DOWN buttons. It was a lift.

Trey hit the UP button and the slow lift clanked its way upwards. The seconds felt like minutes as Trey got angrier and angrier.

"How ungrateful can one person be?" he muttered to himself. Trey literally put his life on the line for his little bro, only for him to be rude and selfish.

Worse than that. He'd betrayed them.

The lift finally stopped. Shutters cranked open, letting in the roaring sound of the factory. Trey leaped out of the lift and ran to his crew, still huddled in a corner by the conveyor belt.

Alvin knew they were here, but he hadn't had his guards escort them out. The aliens thought they were insignificant. Too weak to cause any harm.

He'd show them.

"Trey, what did they do to you?" Dani asked.

Worry creased Madison's face. "Have you seen Layla?"

Trey ignored the questions. "I found Jax and I found the aliens."

Over the roaring sound of machines, Trey told the rest of his crew everything he'd just seen. That the aliens were stealing Earth's greenery. That Jax was on their side. And most surprisingly, that the aliens were tiny.

"Dani, remember the hailstones we saw at school? Those were the aliens. They're the size of mosquitoes!" Trey said.

"It doesn't make sense," Chantelle said. "If they're so tiny, why do they need such colossal amounts of greenery?"

"They say it's for food, but I don't trust them. They've manipulated Jax and now he's acting like some comic book villain," Trey said.

"At least you're safe. But we still need to find Layla," Dani said. "I say we bust out of here and come back with reinforcements. If we scaled the brick wall, we can scale the gate and—"

"No way. I'm not leaving until I've taught those little fleas a lesson," Trey said. He looked around the factory floor for something, anything, that he could use against the aliens.

Dani swapped confused glances with the rest of the crew. "So what if they're tiny? They've taken control of virtually everyone in our neighbourhood! We need an army to take them on."

Finally, Trey's eyes landed on something useful. "Not an army. Just a few of those." He pointed to a trio of fire extinguishers hooked to the wall.

"I thought you said there were thousands of them?" Cameron said.

"Trey, this is not a good idea," Dani said in her most grown-up voice.

"Look. If I can handle Robo-Crankshaw, I can handle the aliens too!" Trey said. He tucked the fire extinguishers under his arm and strode towards the tiny lift.

"But you didn't do that alone!" she yelled after him. "We did it together. As a team."

Trey crawled into the lift and piled the fire extinguishers in beside him. "I've got this, Dani."

Trey's heart raced as the lift descended. He was more nervous than he'd ever been in his life. Stage fright was nothing compared to this.

But he knew that he had the element of surprise on his side. The aliens would never expect Trey to come back to their chamber, let alone with weapons. That had to count for something, right?

Also, they were tiny. "They're just little mosquitoes, OK?" Trey muttered to himself. "Of course I can take them on."

The lift stopped abruptly. Trey clutched the fire extinguisher close. As soon as the shutters lifted, he crawled out of the lift and stepped into the hot, humid chamber.

The aliens were nowhere to be seen. Pinkish

light from the setting sun filtered through the dense overgrowth and dappled the ground. It was deathly still. Apart from the gentle whirr of machinery from the factory upstairs, it was absolutely quiet.

Armed with the fire extinguisher, Trey circled the large plant structure in the centre of the room. Jax's throne.

Then something pierced the silence. A sloshing sound, like water splashing in a bathtub. Trey followed the sound to its source, pushing aside thick-stemmed plants. It was coming from the giant plant in the middle of the chamber. He crouched low and moved towards it.

Trey felt a gentle rumble beneath his feet, like standing at a station platform when the train was due to arrive. The rumble grew more intense and the sloshing sound was only getting louder. Something was coming, and Trey made sure he was in prime position to see it. He crept closer to the plant, gently moving aside thick leaves at its base.

He gasped. A thick glass pipe, wider than his head, connected to the base of the plant. Dark green liquid sloshed inside it. But Trey couldn't tell if the liquid was being sucked from the plant or into it.

His question was answered in a few seconds. The rumbling became even louder. Dark green liquid shot through the pipe and was sucked into the base of the plant.

"It's feeding," Trey whispered to himself.

Litre after litre was consumed in seconds. It had an appetite that seemed never-ending.

The more the plant fed, the more it glowed. The leaves and stem illuminated, casting an eerie neon green light over the ground. Then Trey looked closer. It wasn't the plant that was glowing.

It was the aliens inside it.

Trey staggered back in shock. Tiny green aliens were packed closely on to its surface. They were under his nose all along! Before he could change his mind, he took aim with the fire extinguisher. Releasing the pin and pressing down on the nozzle with all his might, he shot foam in every direction.

He had no idea what to expect. But Trey didn't think the foam would hit the green leaves, rebound and hit him square in the face.

"Blergh!" Trey wiped the cold foam from his eyes. It was as though the leaves were protected by some sort of force field that repelled weapons (and foam).

"Trey? Is that you?" Jax yelled from above. "We told you to leave!"

"I'm not giving up that easily!"

Trey needed a new plan. He grabbed the fire extinguisher and smashed it against the glass pipe with all of his might. Small cracks appeared, spurring him on to smash harder.

"Take! That! E! T!" Trey yelled with every bash.

If he wasn't so obsessed with destroying the pipe, Trey would have noticed the faint buzzing sound in the room. He would have noticed the buzzing intensify. And he would have noticed the plant's thick leaves twitch with irritation.

Jax peered down from the top of his plant throne. "Trey, you need to stop!"

Trey's shirt was drenched through with sweat. He'd done it. Small leaks appeared in the glass pipe through which dark green liquid dripped.

"What are you waiting for, Jax? I've cut off their food supply! It's all over for the aliens," Trey yelled. He tossed aside the fire extinguisher and struggled to catch his breath.

The room seemed warmer than ever.

"You don't know what you're messing with. Go, now!" Jax pleaded.

The buzzing grew louder and louder, as though thousands of bees were in the room. Trey could catch the sound of Jax's voice from up above.

"Look, don't hurt him. OK?" Jax said. But he wasn't talking to his brother.

He was talking to the aliens. Trey didn't know how, but Jax was able to communicate with Alvin. And right now, he was bargaining for Trey's life.

Trey had to move fast. The glass pipe was still supplying dark green liquid to the alien plant. He had to finish the job.

He scrambled to find the fire extinguisher, now hidden by the dense undergrowth. "There you are!" Trey exclaimed. At last, he saw a flash of red and lunged towards it.

With the fire extinguisher in his hands, Trey reached his arms high to deliver one final blow. But something caught his wrist and squeezed.

"Ouch!" he yelped, dropping the fire extinguisher.

Trey looked up. A long green tendril curled around his wrist. And it wasn't letting go. Before he could call for help, the tendril launched Trey into the air with so much force he nearly touched the glass ceiling. He nosedived into a giant green leaf, hurtling down from a terrifying height. He landed on the leaf, and it launched him into the air again at the same breakneck speed.

The giant alien plant tossed Trey into the air over and over. Its thick green tendrils swirled like an octopus's tentacles, catching him seconds before he hit the ground, only to propel him back up into the air. It felt like the worst rollercoaster ever.

"Stop, Alvin! You're hurting him!" Jax screamed.

Finally, the giant plant tossed Trey into a heap. He was bruised, battered and felt like he was gonna hurl. He fell back in a daze while the room span around him.

"What the heck were you thinking, Trey? You made Alvin angry!" Jax yelled. He shouted some other things from atop his green leaf throne, but Trey couldn't hear him. The buzzing noise drowned him out.

"Alvin says you should leave before they really do some damage. Go, now!" Jax yelled.

There was no time to waste. Trey scrambled to his feet and staggered towards the tiny lift.

It was hard to tell what was more bruised: Trey's body or his ego.

30

No matter how many times Trey slammed the UP button, the tiny lift didn't move any faster. His heart pounded as he willed it to hurry up.

At last, he made it. The shutters cranked open and Trey leaped out of the lift ... only to fall into the arms of two guards in green overalls. He struggled against them, but their iron grip held him tight.

"Run! The aliens are coming!" he screamed, but his crew were nowhere in sight.

His warning cries were drowned out by

the roaring of machinery on the factory floor. Production never stopped.

The guards lifted Trey and held him by his arms, one on each side. They marched him through a set of double doors into another part of the factory he hadn't seen before.

The sickly scent of warm sugar hit Trey's nostrils immediately. It was nice and comforting for about three seconds, then it began to turn his stomach.

The factory floor was misty with steam rising from giant copper vats. But through the mist, Trey made out arms and legs clad in green overalls. They moved exactly in time across the length of the factory floor.

Trey realized he was in the real part of the sweet factory. Where the green mind-control candies were made.

He squinted through the mist and saw a familiar face. It was one of the dinner ladies from school! Trey nearly called out to her before realizing it was pointless. She was a robot. They all were.

Next to the dinner lady was his neighbour, Mrs Patel. And right next to them was—

"Mum! Dad!" Trey yelled. He couldn't stop himself.

There, on the production line, were his parents in identical green overalls. They didn't react to Trey's screams.

The guards pushed him up a set of winding iron stairs. Struggling against their grip was impossible. Trey had no choice but to obey.

The narrow stairs led to a locked door. One of the guards waved his wristband over an electronic keypad and the light bleeped green.

"Whoooah!" Trey yelped as the guard shoved him into the room. His shoulder was still tender from playing bouncy castle with the giant alien plant.

This room must have been an old office of some sort. Cardboard boxes and filing cabinets were stacked in the corner. It overlooked the factory floor, which he could see through the narrow windows. When the steam cleared, Trey made out huge copper vats of bubbling white goo being stirred by mechanical poles.

He heard the stamp of the guards' boots as they wound their way back down the iron staircase. For a few seconds, all was quiet.

"Trey? Is that you?"

Familiar faces stepped out of the shadows: Dani, Chantelle, Madison, Layla, Cameron and Logan. And they all looked so happy to see him. But their expressions of joy quickly turned to concern when they saw the state of him. His shirt was ripped in several places and his grey trousers were covered in soil.

"Don't worry about me. I saw my parents down there! And a dinner lady, and my neighbour," Trey said.

Dani nodded. "We know. We saw them when the guards bundled us up here. What happened to you?"

"It's a long story," Trey muttered.

"So how many aliens did you destroy? And where's Jax?" Cameron asked.

Trey's mouth went dry. He'd failed his mission. And now he'd have to tell his crew.

"Here's the thing about the aliens..." Trey began.

The rest of the crew listened. Their eyes widened as he described the giant alien plant, and how it tossed him as easily as a ping-pong ball.

"But you said the aliens are tiny," Logan said. "We can take 'em!"

Trey shook his head. "That's what I thought. But that little shell is like armour. They're impossible to destroy individually."

"So what do we do now?" Dani asked.

Trey shrugged. "If we're lucky, maybe the aliens will forget we're here. And we can escape somehow."

Layla shook her head. "I did not risk being carted away in a green van to give up now! We saw what they've got planned. They're shipping mind-control sweets all over the world!"

"And we're the only ones that can stop them," Chantelle said. "Who knows? We might be the only people in our entire neighbourhood not under their control."

Madison nodded. "We have to stop the sweets from getting out of this factory. Otherwise the world will never be the same again!"

Dani sat down next to Trey. "Today we've escaped an army of robo-teachers, scaled a brick wall and taken on a swarm of greedy aliens. And all in our school uniform!"

"My rugby coach says, 'You only fail when

you stop trying'," Logan said. "And the rest of us haven't given up yet."

"But … you didn't see the size of this thing! I was such an idiot to think I could take it on alone," Trey muttered.

Dani smirked. "Yes, you were. But you have Fernhill's most talented crew assembled in front of you. And Logan."

"Hey!" Logan said.

"And we have a swarm of earth-destroying aliens to stop. You can sit here and feel sorry for yourself. Or you can help us make things really difficult for these aliens," Dani said.

Trey looked up at the faces of his crew. How many times had he given them pep talks when things got rough? If someone had a run-in with a teacher in a bad mood, or was bullied by an older kid, or couldn't get a backflip quite right – wasn't he always there telling them to keep their chin up?

The challenge they faced was bigger than anything they'd ever known. Trey had to be by his crew's side.

Dani stood up and extended her hand. "Are you in or out?"

Trey clasped his friend's hand and pulled himself up. "Come on. We've got work to do."

31

Trey stretched his aching muscles while Dani shared the "genius plan" she'd concocted. The crew assembled in front of the narrow window overlooking the factory.

Dani pointed across the factory floor. "You see that white goo in the big copper vats? I reckon that's the molten sugar."

The copper vat tipped over, pouring goo on to flat, rectangular plates. Green-sleeved arms shot out of the mist, dripping tiny bottles of neon green liquid on to the molten sugar. It instantly turned the white goo into bright green, the colour spreading to every corner. The mist changed from white to green-tinged.

"As for that bright green stuff, I think it's the mind-control substance," Dani said. "The aliens are using it to get into people's heads."

The mist cleared enough for them to see the conveyor belt start moving. The green rectangle of liquid sugar set hard and was pushed on to the conveyor belt. It chugged forward, forcing the green sugar sheet through what looked like a shredder. Hundreds of hard green sweets tumbled out from the other side.

"Watch out for that thing!" Dani said, pointing to the shredder. "It's sharp enough to shred any one of us into pieces."

Cameron gulped.

Thousands of individual sweets rolled down a massive slide leading to a giant chute. From there, the sweets appeared to vanish.

Trey remembered the pipe shooting out thousands of wrapped sweets. "Do you think that pipe connects to the other side of the factory?" he asked.

Chantelle nodded. "It must do. Where else could they go?"

"Then our plan is to block the chute. No chute, no sweets," Dani said.

Trey nodded. "And if they don't have the mind-control sweets, they can't keep on stealing earth's greenery. Not without people noticing, anyway. It'll buy us some time."

"Sounds like a plan," Logan said. "But how do we get out of here?"

"There's got to be a way," Trey said. "Everyone, let's get searching."

The room must have been an office when it was a proper sweet factory. The crew moved around old filing cabinets, broken bits of machinery and dusty cardboard boxes full of mouldering paperwork. But there was nothing. There was no brick wall they could scale and no trapdoor to escape from. It was simply a locked room.

"What's the point of a genius plan if we can't get out of here," Dani groaned.

Suddenly, there was a tap on the window. The crew looked up to see Layla's smiling face on the other side of the glass.

Dani ran to the glass. "You mean this window opens?!"

"Yeah, but only the tiniest amount," Layla said. She pushed up the window to reveal a space no bigger than a cat flap. Only a world-class contortionist could fit through that. Or Layla.

Now, she balanced on the extremely narrow balcony that lined the entire factory wall. There was just enough space for her to walk sideways along the balcony, if she kept her back to the wall.

"I can make it to the chute. I just need something to throw in it," she said.

The rest of the crew turned the old office upside down looking for something. A football would have been ideal, but there wasn't one in sight.

"What about this?" Madison asked. She held up an old-fashioned telephone. The type with a round dial.

"My gran has one of those!" Chantelle said.

Dani inspected the retro telephone. "It's heavy and the plastic is solid," she said. "This could block the chute perfectly." She wrapped the cord around the telephone and handed it to Layla through the narrow window.

"Here you go. It's not perfect, but it'll do," Dani said.

Layla tucked the telephone under one arm and began sidling along the balcony. Inch by inch, she made her way closer to the opposite side of the factory. All Trey and his crew could do was watch.

"I feel so helpless," Trey muttered, wishing there was something more he could do.

"Don't be," Dani said. "Layla's the best person for the job by far. She can do this."

After an agonizingly long minute, Layla made it to the other end of the factory. She took aim, heaving both arms into the air with the telephone in her hands. Then she stopped.

"It's too far for her to reach," Chantelle said. "The chute is several metres away!"

She was right. Layla making it to the other side of the factory was only half the job. She also had to block the chute, which was too far away. What seemed like a good idea a few minutes ago now seemed impossible.

"If only I was there," Logan said. "I could make that shot no problem!"

Trey resisted the urge to roll his eyes.

"Uh-oh," Cameron said. "I don't like the look of this."

"Wait. Is she … climbing?" Dani asked.

A series of metal beams and poles at various heights crisscrossed the factory ceiling. The heavy equipment was suspended from these beams so it was definitely secure. But they were very narrow.

With the telephone under one arm, Layla reached her arm forward and held on to the pole above with one hand. The beam in front jutted out from the balcony, so she stepped on to that. She clung to the pole above, which was at chest height, and wriggled her way forward.

"I can't look!" Madison squealed.

"I can't stop looking," Trey said.

Layla stepped gingerly towards the chute until she disappeared into the plume of white-green mist that rose upwards from the factory floor.

Dani counted to ten. Still no sign of Layla.

Suddenly, a figure emerged from the mist.

It was Layla! And she was no longer holding the old telephone. She gave them a giant thumbs-up.

"She did it! She actually did it!" Trey said. He suddenly had a greater appreciation for the time Layla spent in gymnastics rehearsals.

She made her way back along the balcony, moving faster now she was no longer lumbered with a heavy old telephone.

That's when the rest of the crew noticed a crunching sound, like metal on metal. It rose over the roar of the factory floor.

"There's a pile-up!" Chantelle said. The mouth of the chute overflowed with green sweets.

"The workers haven't noticed," Cameron said. They watched as the workers further down the production line continued to make green sweets.

"Help me in!" Layla said through the window. Dani and Trey pulled her through the narrow

window and she stepped to the ground, graceful as ever. The crew whooped and clapped for her while she gave an elaborate bow.

The lights on the factory floor flickered. The crunching sound grew louder and louder.

"What do you think's gonna happen?" Logan asked.

They didn't have to wait long to find out. Green sweets flew from the chute, popping into the air and ricocheting from every surface. The pipe was well and truly stuffed.

Sparks flew from the conveyor belt, but the workers continued production. These robots weren't all that sophisticated, Trey thought.

Out of nowhere, there was a giant BANG. Then everything went black.

32

"Must be a power cut," Dani said. "Excellent!"

Despite the fact they were still locked away, Trey was triumphant. No power meant no more mind-control sweets being made. They'd blocked the aliens' plan, if only for a few minutes.

"Wait a sec," Trey muttered. "If there's no power, then..." He rushed to the locked door and it pushed open with ease. "Oi, we can escape! The keypad's disabled by the power cut."

"Sick!" Dani yelled. She and the rest of the

crew rushed to the door.

Trey held up his hands. "Here's the plan. We go downstairs, quietly. We escape from the factory, quietly. And we don't stop running until we get home. Got it?"

They nodded. Following Trey's lead, they tiptoed down the creaky winding stairs. Luckily, they had the night sky on their side. The only light in the factory came from the stars twinkling through the windows at the very top of the factory walls. The moon cast beams of light across the floor.

Once Trey reached the bottom of the stairs, he slid his back against the wall and made his way towards the double doors on the other side of the factory. It seemed so far away. The factory floor was eerily quiet without the sound of machinery. With everything switched off, the white mist had settled, revealing the sheer number of green-clad workers.

There were hundreds.

They too were completely still. It was as though the power cut had switched them off as well. The workers' heads bowed down and their arms lay by their sides. Trey could almost pretend they were mannequins.

It felt like it was taking an age, but they were nearly there. The double doors led to the other half of the factory, and from there they could run into the car park and scale the iron gates. Freedom was in sight.

"Hey, this is my big bro!" Logan said. He stepped up to one of the workers standing stock-still by the conveyor belt.

"Logan!" Trey hissed. "We can come back for him. We need to move!"

"Wait a sec," Layla said. She too had broken formation and started walking towards the workers. "That one looks just like my dad!"

The rest of the crew couldn't help but follow

suit. By the time Cameron recognized his mum, Trey realized that they weren't listening to his pleas.

Logan waved his hand in front of the worker's face. "Hey, Callum. It's me! C'mon, we're getting you home." He tugged on his arm but the worker didn't move.

"We need to go!" Trey pleaded.

"And leave our family here?" Layla said. "No way!"

Suddenly, the overhead lights flickered. A fuzzy noise filled the cavernous room and a robotic-sounding voice blared over the tannoy.

"Seize ... any ... intruders. Immediately."

The workers' heads shot up at exactly the same time. Hundreds of pairs of glowing green eyes shone in the flickering light, which was only growing brighter. Any chance they had of a secret escape in the dark was lost.

"On the count of three, we run," Trey

whispered. "One … two … three!"

The crew bolted towards the double doors. At the same time, the heads of the workers turned to face them. They slowly marched towards the crew, who ran towards the double doors. Just before they made it through, the doors opened to reveal more advancing workers. They were trapped.

"There's no point trying to escape!" Dani yelled. "They're just gonna catch us up. We need to stop them."

The crew huddled together while workers slowly advanced from all sides, shuffling one step at a time. It was as though they were in need of recharging. But slow as they were, they would make it to the crew eventually.

"How? There are hundreds!" Trey said.

Chantelle pointed to the giant copper vat in the middle of the factory. "If we knock it over at just the right angle, the hot sugar will spill and block their path. Who's the tallest?"

"I am!" Trey and Logan said at the same time. They turned to each other. "No, I am!" they said.

"You both go," Dani said, exasperated. "Work together!"

The pair shimmied up a ladder against the wall and hoisted themselves on to a wide beam running parallel to the ceiling. Sitting on the beam, Trey and Logan shuffled until they were above the bubbling vat of sugar.

"Kick it sideways!" Chantelle yelled. "And hurry!"

The tips of their toes reached the vat while sitting down. Logan and Trey kicked but they weren't strong enough to knock it over.

"We need to build momentum," Trey said. He lowered himself down, gripping the beam with both hands, and swung himself back like a gymnast. His feet hit the copper vat and it toppled slightly. But it wasn't enough.

"Logan! I need you, man," Trey said.

Logan took a deep breath and lowered himself down. They swung back in unison and kicked the copper vat. It rocked even more.

"One more big push!" Trey yelled. The boys swung back with all of their might and crashed into the vat. It tumbled on to its side, and molten liquid sugar started to spill out in all directions.

Logan and Trey helped each other back on to the beam. They watched as the hot liquid spread across the factory floor.

"Move to higher ground!" Chantelle shouted to the rest of the crew. They immediately began climbing on to nearby machinery before the hot sugar caught their feet.

The liquid sugar moved thick and fast, lapping at the soles of the robo-workers' tough boots. It began to set in seconds, turning as clear and hard as glass.

Just as one of the robo-workers got close enough to reach for Dani's ankle, they froze on the spot. The molten sugar had set solid, clinging to the hard boots of each worker.

"They're not going anywhere," Trey muttered. He high-fived Logan and they made their way across the beam and down the ladder.

The workers reached for the boys as they passed, but they were stuck to the solid sugar.

Trey and Logan ran across the shiny surface towards the rest of the crew. Dani and Layla were on ladders while Chantelle, Madison and Cameron huddled on top of the conveyor belt.

"There's still no way for us to escape!" Dani said. "Check out the double doors."

Trey looked over at the double doors, which were now blocked by several robo-workers. Their boots were stuck to the sticky floor, but their arms were very much still functioning. They grappled at the air around them, waiting to grab an unlucky kid.

"We're finished!" Cameron groaned.

Dani looked around the factory wildly. "There must be another set of doors!"

Trey sighed. He didn't want it to come to this. "There's only one other way out. We go down to Room 101."

33

Trey had a plan. It was risky, but it was the only way he could guarantee a safe escape for his crew.

He told them about the air vent in the aliens' chamber. If they climbed up the tall ladder and crawled through the narrow tunnel, they'd make it out of the factory.

"I'll distract Jax and the aliens while you guys escape," Trey said. "Then I'll follow."

That last bit wasn't exactly true, and they all knew it. There was no way the aliens would let Trey escape after the trouble he'd caused.

"Sounds like a plan," Dani said. "We've made it this far. Let's get going, team."

They agreed to take the lift to Room 101 in pairs. Trey and Dani were to go first and the others would follow as quickly as the rickety lift would allow.

Trey and Dani crawled into the lift. He slammed the DOWN button and the metal cube creaked as it made its descent.

"When the lift door opens, I'll go out first and you run towards the ladder. You can't miss it," Trey said.

Dani shook her head. "There's no way I'm leaving you alone with the aliens, pal."

Trey sighed. "Dani, I need you to get the rest of the crew to safety. I'll be right behind you."

The lift door slid open and the pair crawled out. Room 101 looked even creepier in the dark. Stars in the night sky twinkled through the glass ceiling, but the main source of light came from the giant alien plant. It glowed neon-green, radiating an eerie glow across the room.

"Whoa!" Dani whispered, taking in the surroundings. "That thing looks radioactive. And why is it hotter than an oven in here?"

Trey pointed to the ladder leading up to the tunnel entry. "Dani, the air vent is there. Quick!"

Dani hesitated a second before running to the tunnel and shimmying up the ladder.

Suddenly, the leaves at the very top of the giant plant began to rustle. They parted to reveal Jax standing tall. "Welcome back, bro," he said.

Jax had definitely grown a few inches since Trey saw him earlier that evening. No doubt about it. His skin now glowed with a faint neon green tinge, and his armour was covered in tiny green tubes.

Jax flexed his bicep. "It's a real transformation, right?" he said gleefully. "This is Alvin's recipe. Makes me stronger than I'd ever thought possible. And I'll tell you one thing for free: it's a million times tastier than tuna pasta! I've got a gift for you. Here," Jax said, throwing a handful of green sweets in his direction.

"Are you out of your mind? There's no way I'm eating these and turning into a robot!" Trey said.

Jax rolled his eyes. "Stop being so dramatic. Alvin said that you and the rest of the crew are causing trouble. This will keep you out of the way for a few days. It's temporary."

Trey circled the plant until he ended up at the other side of the room. With Jax's back to the lift, he wouldn't notice the rest of the crew crawl out and escape. Hopefully.

He folded his arms and put on his smuggest voice. "Have we really caused that much trouble? Your aliens have travelled millions of light years ... yet their plan is ruined by a few school kids?"

"I've had enough of your attitude!" Jax scowled. "Eat the sweets and Alvin will spare you. If you don't, then there's no telling what they'll do. It's out of my hands."

Trey shook his head. "Nah, I don't believe it. I mean, look at them! They're no bigger than mosquitoes," he said. "What have I got to worry about?"

The buzzing sound in the room intensified. Trey's plan was working so far.

"I'm warning you," Jax said. "Just eat the green sweets and you'll make it out of here."

"I can take them on. Those aliens are nothing more than flies with fancy suits!" Trey yelled.

The buzzing sound deepened and the air in the room began to vibrate. The tiny green aliens rose from the leaves of the giant plant. They rose higher and higher until the entire chamber was filled with neon green pearls.

Then they flew into the centre of the room. They twisted and twirled like a giant tornado. The buzzing sound was deafening.

Trey looked up to see the tiny green aliens transform into a figure towering dozens of feet into the air. It must have been as tall as their tower block.

The buzzing sound soon died down and the tiny green aliens settled into place. The giant figure was crudely shaped like a person. It had a head, two arms, two legs and glowed bright green in the darkness.

Out of the corner of his eye, Trey saw the lift door open. Layla and Chantelle slid out and ran towards the ladder. Trey had to make sure the aliens were too distracted to notice them.

"Is that meant to be a human being?" he scoffed. "Looks more like a snowman to me."

Alvin responded to the insult by punching their fist through the glass ceiling. Trey backed up against the wall to avoid the shards of glass raining down on them.

The alien's giant hand formed several fingers, which reached down and picked Trey up by the waistband of his trousers.

"**WHOAAAAA!**" he yelled. Trey had had quite enough of being thrown about by extra-terrestrials for one day. Before he became the first human to experience an alien wedgie, Alvin tossed him down besides Jax on the green leaf throne.

"That's enough, Alvin," Jax said.

"How did you—" Trey began.

"I can communicate to Alvin without talking. And vice versa," Jax said simply, as if he was explaining how to unlock the front door.

Trey winced at how sore his body felt. He knew he'd be covered in bruises tomorrow morning. If they made it out of here alive. Trey stood up to face his brother, but he only came up to Jax's shoulders.

"Maybe I should be calling *you* little bro," Jax smirked. "Anyway, I just saved your life. A thank you would be nice."

"Thanks," Trey said through gritted teeth. He was too tired and banged up to pretend he meant it.

Jax frowned. "Now, why is it so hard to say thank you? It's OK if someone else saves the day, you know."

Trey sighed. If there was one thing he learned today, it's that he didn't always know best. And that his school uniform wasn't cut out for alien battles.

"You should have seen the rest of our crew out there," Trey said. "We scaled walls, climbed beams, escaped a sea of molten sugar and a whole bunch of robo-workers with freaky green eyes."

Jax's face softened. "I do miss 'em, you know. It's been a boring few days here all alone. Don't get me wrong, I love my new look. But Alvin's sense of humour is a bit weird. And they're rubbish dancers," he laughed.

Trey smiled. "Then come back. We need you. We always needed you! I know we can't exactly match up to the excitement of an alien fleet ... but we do have a real shot at being a killer dance crew. Besides, do you know how much trouble I'm in if Mum and Dad find out I lost you?"

Jax laughed. He sounded more like his old self. "Yeah. You'd be grounded until the next millennium." He cleared his throat. "Er, Alvin?

I've had a great time but I'd better be getting home now," he said.

"What are you playing at, Jax?" Trey said. "We can't just ask to be released from the clutches of thieving aliens."

Jax looked confused. "Why not? I'm their leader, remember."

A creepy sneer formed on Alvin's huge green face. The buzzing died down and a sound like white noise appeared to come from the aliens.

A metallic laugh came from Alvin's wide grin. "Silly child. You were never our leader."

34

Jax's eyes widened. "I wasn't? But you said—"

"We needed a human to help us with our plan," Alvin continued. Speech came from the giant statue but their mouth didn't move. It was incredibly creepy. "You are more intelligent than the average earthling. You fulfilled the role."

"You've got what you want!" Trey yelled. "You've taken all the green in our neighbourhood, so buzz off."

"No!" Alvin yelled, the force of it knocking Trey to his feet. "Earth's green is the most bountiful in the universe. It will fuel our army of trillions."

"Army? What are you talking about?" Jax yelled.

"We need all of earth's green. There's an entire universe waiting to be plundered!" Alvin bleeped.

Trey stood up. "But if you take it all, then you destroy our planet. We don't survive!"

Alvin was silent for a few seconds. "Your point?"

Jax shook his head violently. "I didn't agree to this."

"We do not require your consent, earthling," Alvin said. "Your crew have caused enough trouble. Once we dispose of you, earth will be ours!"

Jax leaned in closer to Trey. "We've got to stop Alvin. We need to cut off the food supply to the nest."

"The nest? Where's that?" Trey said, spinning around.

Jax pointed down. "You're standing on it. There's a pipe at the back. If we disconnect that, it should cause some real damage."

Trey remembered the glass pipe that he tried to smash earlier. That was their food supply. No wonder it made Alvin mad.

But it wasn't just Alvin that relied on the dark green liquid.

Trey looked at the tubes feeding into Jax's armour. "You know what's going to happen, right?"

Jax shrugged. "Doesn't look like I've got much of a choice." He unplugged the tubes feeding into his armour and climbed down the giant leaf.

Covered by the dense green undergrowth, Trey and Jax crouched down and ran towards the neon green pipe.

Jax heaved at the giant pipe, which was still

301

bearing a few dents from Trey's encounter with it earlier. "I'm pulling as hard as I can!" he yelled. "But I'm getting smaller already."

Without Alvin's food pumped into his veins, Jax was visibly shorter, and his muscles were already shrinking.

"At least your skin doesn't have that weird green glow," Trey said.

He joined his brother and pulled too. But it was no use. They weren't going to disconnect the pipe between the two of them.

Trey peeked through the leaves and saw Alvin crashing through the undergrowth, trying to find the two boys. Then he heard a familiar voice.

"Trey? Where are you?" He looked through the giant leaves and was shocked to see his friends! Chantelle, Layla, Madison, Logan and Cameron climbed back down the ladder.

"I told them to escape," Trey muttered. But

he couldn't have been happier to see them.

Trey stuck his hand out of the undergrowth and waved madly, hoping one of them would see him. Dani noticed and led the squad through the dark leaves to the pipe.

"What are you doing here?" Trey demanded.

Jax looked shocked. "You came back for us? Even after what I did?"

"We heard screams! There's no way we could escape without all of our crew," Dani said.

"What can we do?" Logan asked.

"Distract Alvin!" Trey said. His friends looked confused. "You know, the giant alien out there hell-bent on taking over the world?"

Madison's face lit up. "We can distract Alvin, all right!" She yanked out a large fern from the ground and told the others to do the same.

While Trey and Jax pulled on the tube with all of their might, they watched as their friends formed a plan to distract the giant alien.

Following Madison's lead, they quickly disguised their clothes with giant ferns, stuffing the huge leaves into their waistbands and down the back of their shirts.

"Layla, you go on Logan's shoulders!" Madison yelled. "And Chantelle, you do the same with Cameron."

"What ... on earth ... are you playing at?" Jax said while catching his breath. Dismantling this pipe was no joke.

"All those tiny aliens came together to form one big alien, right?" Madison said. "Well, so can we!"

Trey paused. "That's the most ridiculous thing I've ever heard. And it might just work."

Layla and Chantelle linked arms from atop Logan and Cameron's shoulders. Dani and Madison positioned themselves behind them, clutching their ferns.

"Chaaaaaaarge!" Madison yelled. As they

toppled towards Alvin, they waved their ferns and roared menacingly. In the dim light of Room 101, the six friends did look like a multi-limbed being from another planet.

Alvin swatted at them, but they held strong.

"Wow. It actually worked!" Trey said.

"No time to stop. Pull like your life depends on it!" Jax said.

They both grabbed a length of the pipe and heaved it slowly away from the giant alien plant, inch by inch.

The buzzing sound was now at an ear-splitting level, high-pitched and desperate.

"It's working!" Trey yelled. Dark green liquid oozed around the edges.

Finally, the pipe dislodged with a pop. More dark green liquid swooshed through the pipe and spilled on to the ground.

Suddenly, the giant alien plant above them crumpled in on itself. The colour faded from

rich green to dusty grey, and the rubbery leaves deflated before their eyes.

Trey and Jax ran out of the undergrowth.

"Did it work?" Dani yelled.

Before anyone could answer, they looked up at the towering neon green figure above them. The air around Alvin vibrated and the tiny green aliens started tumbling to the floor in their thousands.

"To the tunnel!" Trey shouted.

Layla and Chantelle dismounted, then they all ran towards the ladder leading to the air vent tunnel. One by one, they hoisted themselves upwards and crawled through the tunnel.

Trey was the last to go up the ladder. Once he reached the mouth of the tunnel, he turned around to see the carnage before him.

The giant alien plant had disintegrated into grey dust, as well as the rest of the foliage. Neon green aliens littered the ground, which was now sodden with dark green liquid.

"Trey, let's go!" Jax yelled, waiting for his brother.

But Trey didn't move. He had to know they'd vanquished the aliens for good. Otherwise, what was the point in trying to escape?

They watched as the aliens vibrated on the ground, their buzzing and bleeping filling the chamber.

"Don't worry, bro. Alvin's finished," Jax said.

Suddenly, the aliens began to glow again. Then they moved. Like a magnet collecting iron filings, the aliens zipped together to form a giant column.

Trey's heart raced. "You sure about that?"

The thousands of aliens now formed what looked like a cone, with a nozzle pointing towards the sky. The neon green aliens sparkled and shone in the darkness.

It happened so quickly they couldn't quite

believe their eyes. The neon green cone began to rumble and levitate. Then it shot through the glass ceiling and into the sky, leaving nothing but green-tinged fumes in its wake.

"It's a rocket!" Trey said.

Jax clapped his hand on Trey's shoulder. "Something tells me that Alvin is gone for good."

35

The next day came and went without a single person mentioning the strange events of the past week. No one seemed to remember being turned into a robot or being forced to work in the factory. Trey and Jax's parents came home the next day with no memory of the weekend.

Sure, the workers in green overalls were confused to find themselves in the factory with their boots stuck to the floor. But by the time they made it home and went to bed, they were already starting to forget, and they couldn't remember a thing in the morning. Logan must've asked his brother one hundred times if he'd been in the old abandoned factory, and he had no memory of it.

"Don't you think it's annoying that we saved the entire neighbourhood, possibly the world, and no one remembers it?" Trey said to Dani and Jax on the way to school. A month had passed since they first saw the green flash.

Dani chuckled. "Yeah, a bit of credit would be nice. If my mums knew what we went through to save them all, maybe they'd get me a new phone."

"Is their allotment back to normal, yet?" Jax asked.

Even though the effect of the mind-control coffee and candies wore off not long after the aliens left, Earth's green would take longer to restore. The lawn in the local park was still patchy and grey, the hedges dry and dusty. But green patches were starting to peek through. Progress was slow, but it was happening.

"It's getting there," Dani sighed. "Mum and Ma still expect a bumper crop of kale. Lucky me," she added sarcastically.

"Cheer up, Dani," Trey said. "At least it's not spabbages!"

Jax stopped walking. "That reminds me, Trey! I'm gonna be a bit late to rehearsal tonight. Mrs Appleby needs a hand with the allotment again."

Since Jax felt guilty about everything he had apparently done to assist the aliens, he vowed to help the caretaker restore her spabbages to their former glory. It was the least he could do after she risked everything to save them from the robo-teachers.

Like the rest of the school, Ms Appleby didn't remember a thing about that bizarre week. She simply assumed that Jax had taken an interest in growing green vegetables.

Trey raised one eyebrow. "I'm starting to think you like gardening more than dancing, bro."

"Hey, we should just be grateful Jax isn't obsessed with Area51.com any more," Dani said.

"Listen! My so-called obsession saved all of us. We'd be robots on a grey, dusty planet if it weren't for me," Jax said.

"And then we saved you. So, let's call it even, eh?" Trey said.

The trio neared the school gates. Even now, one month later, they still scanned the schoolyard for bright green vending machines. But Park View High School seemed back to normal.

The school bell rang and everyone began making their way to lessons.

Dani waved goodbye. "See ya at rehearsal tonight!"

"But it's Tuesday. Don't you have Triple F's practice tonight?" Trey asked.

"I got them to change the schedule so I could still perform with Fly High Crew," Dani said. "Can't expect you to win the Summer Talent Show without me!"

Trey smiled. "Sweet. See you tonight."

As soon as his last lesson of the day was over, Trey raced to the PE hall for Fly High Crew rehearsals. It still surprised him how little had changed. The hall still smelled faintly of bleach and rubber mats, Ms Tackle still waved hello at the start of every rehearsal, and the space in the hall was still tight as ever.

But this time, the Fly High Crew had some new members.

Madison, Cameron and Layla might not be street dancers. But Trey realized he couldn't let their skills go to waste.

Why were Madison's superstar trampolining skills or Cameron's epic roundhouse kicks not being put to good use in their routine? And he had to find a place for Layla's exceptional agility.

Logan was the latest addition to the crew. Once he realized he could do rugby *and* street dance, the rest of Fly High Crew were happy to welcome him. Sure, he'd been a pain in the past, but he'd more than made up for it in the factory. And he wasn't all that graceful on his feet. But he was dedicated and a quick learner.

Trey wound his way through the cramped PE hall until he found his friends. They lay on the rubber mats, stretching their limbs in preparation for rehearsal.

"Jax is running late today so I thought we'd

try something different," Trey said.

Logan narrowed his eyes. "How different? 'Cause I'm only just getting the hang of this routine."

"Our routine is missing something, but I don't know what. I can't figure it out alone," Trey said. He sat down on the mat and took a notebook from his rucksack. "So, I want to hear your ideas."

"Are you serious?" Chantelle asked.

Dani leaned in. "Is this the real Trey speaking?"

Trey smiled. "Listen, I know I haven't been all that keen on sharing ideas in the past. But you lot have skills. And Fly High Crew is going to need all the help we can get for this talent show."

By the time the crew finished sharing their ideas, Trey had covered several pages of paper with notes and ideas. The routine for the talent show looked a little different to how it looked last month. But after hearing their ideas, Trey couldn't imagine doing it any other way.

36

The audience clapped politely as the next act at the Summer Talent Show took the stage. Trey peeked through the backstage curtains and took in the rows of people. He gulped. He'd never seen the school auditorium so full.

Trey headed back to his crew, who were warming up. They were wearing the matching green T-shirts with a Fly High Crew logo sketched by Chantelle. This wasn't a normal performance, so normal clothes wouldn't do.

It was their first proper show and their

biggest audience ever. Trey couldn't lie: a small part of him would rather face Alvin again then perform onstage. But that was the pre-show nerves talking, he told himself.

Ms Tackle approached them with a clipboard. "You're on next, Fly High Crew!"

Chantelle took deep breaths. "Oh, boy," she said. "These butterflies in my tummy need to give it a rest."

"Don't worry," Cameron said. "We smashed it in rehearsals and this is no different."

"I'm good with most of the routine. But that finale? It doesn't always go to plan," Logan said.

He had a point. The final part of their routine was a dance move that was pretty risky. When it worked, it was spectacular. But for that to happen, every member of the crew had to give it their all. There was no room for error.

Trey leaned in towards the crew. They

formed a semi-circle around him. "Listen, gang. Remember what I always say? If we can take on a giant alien, then—"

"We can take on the Summer Talent Show," his friends finished the sentence in unison and giggled.

"How could we forget? You've said it every say for the last month," Jax said.

"You get my point, though. This talent show is light work," Trey said, even as his own heart was racing.

The sound of the audience clapping filtered through to the backstage area.

"Fly High Crew, you're up!" someone yelled.

As the crew shuffled to the stage, they bumped into Mrs Upton and Mr Crankshaw. The pair were monitoring the backstage area along with some volunteers.

"Break a leg, children!" Mrs Upton said.

Mr Crankshaw sneered. "Yes. Please do," he muttered.

"Thanks, Mrs Upton," Trey said. "We'll try our best!"

The crew followed Trey on to the stage as the audience welcomed them with light applause. He noticed his family had seats in the front row: Mum, Dad and even Nate! He resisted the urge to smile or wave. Then, the stage lights flicked on and he couldn't see anything but the white lights. The crew assumed their positions and bowed their heads.

The thumping electronic beat bounced out of the speakers, way louder than in rehearsal. But as soon as he heard the familiar music, Trey's nerves disappeared. Their heads shot up and their arms flew into the air, their bodies jolting in perfect time to the bass.

The mass of bodies on the stage moved as one. But the genius of their routine was that everyone worked to their unique strengths. Layla wowed the crowd with a back handspring while Logan lifted Madison on to his shoulders. From there, she stood up and leaped gracefully into the arms of her crew. Trey and Jax caught her, helping Madison to her feet.

Once again, Trey felt ridiculously proud of his crew. Layla, Madison, Cameron and Logan only started dancing a month ago, but their hard work was paying off. They were every bit as good as the original crew.

The music morphed into a catchy hip-hop beat that had the audience on their feet, clapping along. The crew's routine changed too, from front flips and b-twists that defied gravity, to a choreographed piece inspired by Cameron's karate drills. They high-kicked and chopped to the music before assuming their position for the finale. Trey took a deep breath. It was now or never...

In a flash, the crew zipped into place, jumping on shoulders to form a human pyramid. Logan and Trey held firm at the base while Layla and Chantelle sat on their shoulders. They locked arms while the rest of the crew positioned themselves on either side of Logan and Trey. Moving as one, their arms shot into the air at the exact moment that the music reached its crescendo. It was faultless.

For a split-second, there was silence. Trey could only hear the sound of his heartbeat racing.

Then the audience burst into a round of applause so loud it startled him. They whooped and clapped and stamped their feet.

The crew helped Layla and Chantelle down, then they turned to face their audience. They bowed before running off-stage.

Their T-shirts were sticky with sweat and they desperately needed a glass of water. But the Fly High Crew were ecstatic. Like Trey, they couldn't stop smiling.

"We did it!" Jax yelled. "That finale was sick."

"It's the best we've ever done it!" Dani said.

"Bravo, children!" Mrs Upton said. "That was a stellar performance and you all made a brilliant team. In all my years running the Summer Talent Show, I've never seen anything like it. Wouldn't you agree, Mr Crankshaw?"

Mr C stood next to the head teacher, silently seething. His face was a shade of dark red that Trey's mum would have called "puce". "Yes. It was quite something," he said through gritted teeth.

"Cheers, Miss!" Jax said. "We rehearsed super hard."

"Speaking of rehearsals, Ms Tackle said that you were having some problems securing a regular practice space?" Mrs Upton said.

Mr C jumped in. "I'm merely concerned about health and safety. The PE hall is rather cramped, head teacher."

"Understood. Leave it with me, children," Mrs Upton said. "I guarantee you will have a decent rehearsal space just in time for the summer holidays."

Trey's eyes widened. "Seriously, Miss?"

"Rehearsing in school over the summer holidays? T-that is most unorthodox..." Crankshaw stuttered.

"Oh, but it's absolutely necessary. This crew is full of our brightest talents, Mr Crankshaw. They simply must practise!"

The crew grinned at one another. Finally, they had a rehearsal space sorted.

"But there'd be no one to supervise or patrol the school grounds. It's a security nightmare!" Crankshaw said, his face turning an even deeper red.

Mrs Upton sighed. "As you're so concerned with security, you can stay on the school grounds while they rehearse. Every single Tuesday throughout the summer holidays."

Jax smiled cheekily. "Um, actually, Miss, I think we need to rehearse more than that. Three times per week should do the trick!"

Mrs Upton clapped her hands together. "Then that's settled! Mr Crankshaw, see me in my office next week to discuss the schedules. And, children? If you need anything else, don't hesitate to ask," she said before walking away.

Crankshaw glared at the crew. For a second, Trey could have sworn his eyes flashed green. A chill quickened through his veins as Trey instantly recalled his memories of escaping from the robo-teachers. This couldn't be happening.

But then the green flash went as quickly as it appeared.

Would you listen to yourself? Trey thought.

You're getting carried away, just like Jax.

Mr Crankshaw walked away without saying anything. It must have all been in Trey's head.

"And now, it's time to announce the winners of Park View's Summer Talent Show!" a voice boomed.

"All performers to the stage, please!" A volunteer with a clipboard yelled.

The Fly High Crew joined the dozens of performers and squashed themselves onstage. Dani and Chantelle held hands while Logan took deep calming breaths. For some reason, Trey felt just as nervous when they were about to perform.

They stood behind the host, a sixth form student who loved the sound of his own voice too much and wore a sparkly jacket just for the occasion.

"In my hand, I hold the name of the winners of this year's Summer Talent Show!" he yelled and everyone clapped.

"Come on, man," Jax muttered. "Spill it!"

"In third place, we have superstar songstress Serena Jackson!"

The audience cheered as Serena bowed and took her trophy.

"In second place, we have..." The host paused for effect. "The Original Rebels!"

Trey deflated as the talent show's only other dance troupe ran up and accepted their trophy. Surely the school wouldn't give prizes to two sets of dancers?

"It's the one you've been waiting for," the host began.

Trey looked over at his crew and smiled. "Don't sweat it," he mouthed.

"The winner of the Park View Summer Talent Show is..."

Trey closed his eyes. Why did these few seconds feel like hours?

"The Fly High Crew!" the host yelled. The audience jumped to their feet and the sound of their applause crashed down on Trey like a tidal wave.

The crew jumped into each other's arms, screaming and shouting with joy. Trey blinked.

They'd actually won?

"C'mon, let's get our trophy!" Dani said, pushing Trey to the front of the stage. They got there just in time for him to see Crankshaw stomp out of the auditorium.

"How does it feel to win first prize?" the host asked, pushing his mic in their faces.

"Incredible!" Jax yelled.

"Fantastic!" Dani shouted.

Trey couldn't deny that winning felt amazing. The Fly High Crew had worked really hard for this.

"It feels great," Trey said. "But dancing with my crew felt even better!"

Dani grinned. "I know exactly what you mean," she whispered to him.

The Fly High Crew stood in a row and took their final bow together while the audience whooped and cheered. Jax waved to Mum, Dad and Nate in the front row.

Trey looked over at his friends and grinned. There was no place he'd rather be.

ASHLEY BANJO is the founder of street dance collective Diversity (winners of **BRITAIN'S GOT TALENT** in 2009), a creative director for many TV shows, a TV presenter and judge on hugely popular shows such as **DANCING ON ICE** and **BRITAIN'S GOT TALENT.**

JORDAN BANJO is a key member of Diversity and has presented **THE GREATEST DANCER.** He is the current **KISS FM** Breakfast Show presenter with Diversity member Perri Kiely.

They are passionate about reaching kids through their storytelling on stage and now on the page.

🐦 @ASHLEYBANJO @JORDAN_BANJO
📷 @ASHLEYBANJOGRAM @JORDBANJO

ALEXANDRA SHEPPARD is a social media strategist by day and writer by night. She is the author of *Oh My Gods.*

🐦 @ALEXSHEPPARD
📷 @ALEXSHEPPARD19

Photo © Kareem Thompson

DIONNA GARY-BUNN is a Visual Artist from
New Jersey with a degree in Graphic design and
over 8 years of experience within Branding &
Illustration work. Her artwork represents cultural
diversity and seeing herself in her art. Dionna's goal
is to tell a story through her artwork and to fill
a space with something beautiful.

@DESIGNEDBYDG

ACKNOWLEDGEMENTS

Between us we have so many inspirations and people we're thankful for, both for this story and in our general lives. But we wanted to firstly thank each other! We're together on this wicked new journey of becoming authors! We can't wait to see what the future holds for this new creative journey. Secondly and most importantly we dedicate it to our beautiful children, Cassius and Mayowa and Rose and Micah. Hopefully you will all read this book one day and we hope you enjoy it as much as we did creating it! Becoming dads has given us a whole new perspective and we love you more than words could ever express!

A huge thank you to our amazing writer Alexandra Sheppard who truly brought our vision to life. Every step of this book was a joy and Alex was a massive part of that. And finally, we wouldn't be here without our mum and dad for obvious reasons but we wouldn't be who we are without them either. They're our biggest inspirations and our biggest fans, thank you Mum and Dad, always love, none of this is possible without you two.

ASHLEY AND JORDAN

STREET DANCE MOVES FOR YOU TO LOOK UP AND LEARN!

B-TWIST

ELBOW FREEZE

SIX STEP

CORK

FRONT FLIP

SIDE TUCK

WINDMILL

AIRFLARE

APPLEJACK

BACKSPIN

SWIPES

EYES
TO THE
SKIES...
FOLLOW
THE GLOW!
#FLYHIGHCREW